GW00649995

Typewriter Pub, an imprint of Blvnp Incorporated
A Nevada Corporation
1887 Whitney Mesa DR #2002
Henderson, NV 89014
www.typewriterpub.com/info@typewriterpub.com

ISBN: 978-1-64434-275-6

DISCLAIMER

This book is a work of fiction. The characters, incidents, and dialogue are
drawn from the author's imagination and are not to be construed as real.
While references might be made to actual historical events or existing
locations, the names, characters, places, and incidents are either products
of the author's imagination or are used fictitiously, and any resemblance to
actual persons living or dead, business establishments, events or locales is
entirely coincidental.

A DEADLY TRIP

Sequel to The Subway

JAE JAE

type
writer
pub

To my mother and my readers.
Because of you, I was able to bring this book to life.

CHAPTER ONE

Despite the number of people currently crammed like sardines in a can in the small gymnasium, it was freezing inside.

Freezing and quiet.

It was so quiet one could have heard a feather drop, but I assumed that was just how he liked it.

"He's not going to do it."

"He is."

"Come on. Even *he* has more sense than that."

"I'm telling you, he's going to do it."

"No way."

"Just wait and see."

Megan and I turned our heads and watched expectantly as the speaker climbed up the few sets of steps to the stage before stopping in front of the podium. There was a brief pause. As if they were waiting until all eyes were on them and that they had everyone's undivided attention, before they cleared their throat to start reading from the paper they had placed on the podium.

"I'd like to say that I enjoyed my time here at Colton High, but if I do, then I'd be lying, and my mother didn't raise me to be a liar."

I turned to see Megan's jaw hit the ground. I just shook my head and smiled before returning my attention to the speaker.

"I don't know if there's anyone ready to see Colton High in their rearview mirror more than me. So, I'm not going to stand up here and go on and on about how I'll miss this school and everyone here because then I'd be lying again, and as I said, my mom didn't raise me to be a liar. I don't want to stand up here talking all day, either. That'd be a waste of everyone's time. Because let's be honest, who wants to sit in this hot gym and listen to someone drone on about the good old days of high school? No one. So, instead, I'd like to leave you with this quick and simple phrase. I'll sum up everything in a few short sentences before I take my seat."

There was another pause and then—

"Goodbye, seniors. Goodbye, class. Colton High School, you can kiss my—"

"Okay!"

I watched in amusement as our school's principal, Ms. Stanley, ran up on stage. She almost tripped in her heels before quickly snatching the microphone away from the speaker.

"Thank you, Mr. Daniels, for such an . . . enlightening speech," she said after shooting him a glare.

Archer gave her a mock salute before descending the stairs and casually made his way back to his seat next to me.

I turned to look at him before leaning over and whispering, "Nice speech."

He smirked. "You think so? I stayed up all night working on that one."

"Oh yeah, I could definitely tell."

Megan leaned forward to say, "Would it have killed you to make an effort and prepare a real speech?"

Archer pretended to think about it for a few seconds before replying, "Yes, it would've, and we all know you'd miss me most of all if I died."

I watched, smiling, as Megan's face turned a light shade of red.

Since Archer and I had started dating, I might have mentioned to him that Megan had an infatuation with him, and

2

ever since then, Archer went out of his way to speak to her just to see her get all flustered.

"Would not," Megan said, trying to sound serious but failing miserably.

"Are you saying you wouldn't care if I died?" Archer put a hand to his heart and pretended to look hurt.

Apparently, Megan thought he was actually upset. "No, I-I didn't mean that . . . I would . . . but you . . . and . . . I wouldn't . . ."

I placed my hand on Megan's shoulder. "Meg, he's messing with you," I said, fighting the laughter threatening to break through my smile.

Megan's face turned an even darker shade of red as she folded her arms and quickly turned around.

I turned back to Archer.

"You're going to give her a heart attack one day and kill her, and unfortunately for you, that means I'll have to kill you too."

Archer opened his mouth to reply, but just then, an annoyingly high-pitched voice spoke from in front of us.

"Could you keep it down back there? Some of us are *trying* to listen."

I scowled at the face of Avery Robinson as she scrunched her face up at me.

"If you don't get her, I will," I warned Archer quietly without breaking eye contact with the she-demon.

As soon as it became known to the public that Archer and I were together, she became public enemy number one. She was constantly sending me dirty looks in the halls and saying petty things to her friends when I was within earshot. Like, "Can you believe Archer is with her? Talk about a downgrade." or "We all know he only wants one thing, and once he gets it, he'll come crawling back to me."

That type of nonsense.

I'm not the type of person to let those kinds of things get to me, but one day I caught Avery basically trying to shove herself

3

down Archer's pants in the hallway during lunch, and I kid you not, I almost killed her.

Lucky for Archer, when I caught them, he seemed like he had actually been trying to stop her. Otherwise, we would have had a joint funeral for both of them that day.

Ever since that day, Archer made me promise that I wouldn't try anything like that again because he didn't want me getting into trouble or some nonsense like that. I can't really say that I remember because I wasn't listening to him then.

I was too busy picturing Avery's head underneath a steamroller with me at the wheel. Anyway, I had kept my promise so far, but Avery was starting to test my limits.

"Just ignore them," said yet another annoying and familiar voice.

I turned my scowl to the back of Cade Phillips' head.

Coward.

He didn't even have the guts to turn around and look at us. It probably was because he was scared Archer would break his nose again. But, hey.

After catching his best friend and his girlfriend together in the old bathrooms at school five months earlier, Archer had dumped Avery and punched Cade in the nose, breaking it as a result. And rightfully so, might I add.

Surprisingly, Avery and Cade were still together. I wondered how long it would last before she was caught in the bathroom with someone else. So far, they were still going strong, or whatever it was you wanted to call it.

Avery shot me one last nasty look before turning back around.

I simply shook my head and returned my attention to Ms. Stanley.

"I'd like to say how much I've enjoyed having you all here at Colton High for the past few years. I've come to know many of you so well. Some of you more so than others." At that, she shot a look at Archer directly, and you could hear the laughter from the students around us. "But I feel like a parent who has watched all her children grow up."

"Bullshit." Archer coughed loudly into his fist, causing everyone within earshot to snicker. I quickly elbowed him and shot him a look.

"I'm so proud of all of you and see nothing but the best for your future endeavors," Ms. Stanley continued. "Congratulations, Class of 2021!"

Cheers went up all around as everyone stood and started clapping. Almost simultaneously, as if everyone was reading each other's minds, we threw our caps into the air, and the cheers grew louder.

This was it. We made it.

No more high school. No more lunches that resembled prison food, looked inedible, and tasted awful. No more snobby Avery and her pack of hyenas.

We were starting our lives out in the real world, and I couldn't have been more excited.

There was nothing but good things ahead.

At least, that's what I thought at first.

CHAPTER TWO

"This is it. My life is over!"

I fell to the floor and covered my eyes with the back of my hand.

"Oh, the pain! The horror!"

"Gemma."

"What am I going to do?!"

"Gemma." The voice persisted.

"This is it! The end of Gemma Conners as you know it!"

"Gemma!"

I slowly opened one eye to peek up at my mom.

"Yes?"

"I found your swimsuit. It's right here."

My mom held up my new blue and black polka-dotted bikini that I'd been looking for the last hour.

"How'd you find it? I looked everywhere for that thing," I asked as I quickly stood up to take the bikini from my mom.

"It was in your closet."

"What?! I checked the closet three times and couldn't find it anywhere."

"Hmm." My mom gave me that look. The one all moms give their kids when they didn't believe a word they were saying.

"I did," I exclaimed, trying to convince her.

"I'm sure you did. Now, are you all packed?" my mom asked, eyeing my overstuffed suitcase.

I walked over to my bed, where my suitcase was laid, and tossed the bikini inside before struggling to zip it up.

Once zipped up, I turned to face my mom with a smile.

"I'm all packed."

I was beyond excited for this week. Tomorrow I'd be leaving, with the rest of my senior class, to spend a week in Hawaii for our senior class trip. I had been looking forward to this day almost as much as I had been to graduating.

"You didn't forget anything, did you? You have your toothbrush, extra underwear, socks—"

"Mom, for the hundredth time, I have everything. Okay? Stop worrying," I said, cutting her off.

My mom sighed before nodding.

"Besides, shouldn't you be starting on dinner?" I checked the clock on my nightstand, which read 5:30 PM. "Archer should be here soon."

My mom's eyes widened as she noticed the time.

"Oh my goodness! You're right!" My mom turned and quickly rushed out of the room. A few seconds later, I heard her hurried footsteps running down the stairs.

I smiled and shook my head.

My mom had been begging me to invite Archer over for dinner before we left for our trip. She had convinced herself this was the last time she'd be able to have dinner with her 'son-in-law,' as she liked to call him, for a while.

I kept telling her we would only be gone for a week. Then we would be back for the rest of the summer until college started when both Archer and I would attend NYU. But she was having none of it.

I dragged my heavy suitcase off the bed and sat it near my closet before heading back and plopping down on my bed with a sigh.

7

I could not believe I would be in college in just a few months. I remember only a few months ago I wasn't even sure if I would see daylight again. I tried to keep that memory buried as far as I could in the back of my mind, but sometimes, like when I went to sleep at night, I couldn't help but relive it.

I stayed in my room, seated on my bed, trying to think of only the good to come in the future until I heard the doorbell ring.

I checked the time. It was now a little after 6:30 PM. Time sure does fly when one was trying not to relive a hellish nightmare.

I hopped out of bed ready to head downstairs but not before stopping in front of my mirror to check my appearance.

I had recently made the decision to cut my hair. So now, instead of reaching the middle of my back, it stopped just below my shoulders. I had even started curling it. A skill that I was proud to say I had learned, so it no longer fell into a lifeless black sheet but had a little volume.

I glanced at my outfit—a simple green baby-doll shirt, a pair of black dress pants, and a pair of black flats.

Usually, I wouldn't be caught dead in anything besides jeans, T-shirts, or hoodies. But because my mom had gone to so much trouble over this dinner and demanded that I wear appropriate dinner clothes, I had no choice.

I took a deep breath before hurrying down the stairs to answer the front door. When I opened it, I was greeted by the sight of none other than Mr. Archer Daniels himself in all his gorgeous glory.

He gave me a breathtaking smile as soon as he saw me, which I returned happily.

Dressed in a black button-down shirt—sleeves rolled up to just above his elbows—and dark-washed jeans, he looked *silently gorgeous*. It was what I liked to call people who were too good-looking for words.

His green eyes were as stunning as ever, and his dark brown hair was stylishly messy.

Yep, definitely silently gorgeous.

He remained smiling as he eyed me up and down. "You look beautiful."

I felt my face heat up at the compliment. I still wasn't used to receiving them. "Thanks."

But leave it to him to ruin a compliment.

"I mean, you don't look as good as me, but you come in at a close second," he teased.

I rolled my eyes, standing aside so he could come in.

"Shut up and come in before I tell my mom you got hit by a bus and couldn't make it."

"That's not very nice," he stated as he walked in.

"Yeah, well. I've never claimed to be a very nice person," I countered as I closed the door.

"Honey, who was at the door? Was it Archer?" my mom called from the kitchen.

"Yeah, it's him!" I called back.

She stuck her head out of the doorway to the kitchen and waved at Archer, spoon still in her hand.

"Hi, Archer! Dinner will be ready in a few minutes."

He waved back, and being the charmer he was, he then tilted his head up and sniffed the air dramatically.

"Whatever you're cooking in there, Mrs. Conners, smells delicious. If your food tastes like it smells, I'm sure you could make dishwater taste good."

To my surprise, my mom actually blushed!

"Oh, Archer. You're too sweet," she replied with a small laugh.

"I think I'm going to be sick," I mumbled.

"I'm already allowing you to date my daughter. Now you're trying to steal my wife too?"

I turned to see my dad standing in the entryway to the living room, glaring at Archer. It was safe to say that Archer and my dad did not have the best relationship. It wasn't because of anything Archer had done. My dad just did not like the idea of me being within a five-foot radius of any male.

Archer rubbed the back of his neck nervously.

"Ugh. No, sir?" he said, but it came out sounding more like a question.

I had to admit it *was* nice to see somebody make Archer so nervous.

"Oh, John, leave him alone. You're making him nervous," my mom admonished.

My dad folded his arms across his chest and replied, "Good." Before heading into the kitchen.

My mom just shook her head.

"Don't worry about him. He's all bark and no bite." My mom smiled in reassurance before going back to the kitchen.

"Your dad hates me," he said, shaking his head.

"I know."

Archer looked at me with wide eyes. "You're not supposed to agree!"

I smiled and shrugged my shoulders. "There's no point in lying to you. He hates you."

He ran a hand down his face and groaned.

I walked up to him and wrapped my arms around his waist.

"All you have to do is make it through this one dinner and then it's you and me in Hawaii."

His face brightened at that as he looked down at me. "Right. Just get through this dinner," he said in a subdued voice, trying to reassure himself.

"Yep, everything should be fine . . . you know, as long as you don't die from food poisoning from eating my mom's cooking, of course," I added as I let go of him and skipped into the kitchen, leaving a gawking Archer behind.

CHAPTER THREE

Dinner was definitely intriguing, and it didn't have anything to do with my mom's cooking. She had actually made a decent meal of spaghetti bolognese, garlic bread, and salad without managing to set the food or herself on fire.

Even though her cooking was clearly a miracle it, wasn't what made dinner so interesting. No, what made it so was the two males currently sitting at the dinner table.

My dad was staring daggers at Archer, who looked as if he would like nothing better than to be anywhere but here.

"So, Arthur . . ." Dad began.

"It's Archer . . . sir."

"Right. So, Artie. What are your plans now that you've graduated?"

Archer shot me a look before clearing his throat. "Ugh. I plan on going to college."

"Interesting. Where exactly do you plan on going?"

"NYU."

"Hmm, what a coincidence. Gemma is attending NYU too." My dad turned to my mom and gave her a fake smile. "Isn't that just great?"

She gave my dad one of her stares before she turned to Archer and gave him a genuine smile.

"I think it's fantastic that you're both attending college together. This way, I'll have somebody to look after my Gemma."

11

I covered my face with my hand and groaned. "Mom, I don't need anyone to look after me."

"You're saying that now, but what happens when one of your classes is across campus, and you have to walk there by yourself, or you have to walk back at night?"

"Mooom."

My mom held her hands up placatingly. "I'm just saying it'll be nice to have someone to watch out for you, is all."

"So, Archie," my dad began again.

I knew Dad was saying Archer's name wrong on purpose, just to get under Archer's skin, but fortunately, he didn't even seem fazed by it.

"What do you plan on majoring in?"

"Prelaw, sir."

I swear my dad's left eye twitched as his gaze slowly slid over to me. "Would you look at that? Another. Coincidence," he bit out. "Gemma wants to major in prelaw as well."

It was news to me. I had no idea what he was planning on majoring in until a few seconds ago. I was constantly asking him about it, but he always evaded the question.

I turned to him in surprise. "Really? You're interested in law?"

He actually looked embarrassed. "Ugh, yeah. I wanted to tell you, but I didn't want you to think that I was choosing the same major as you just to follow you or something. We're not *that* kind of couple."

"Could've fooled me," my dad muttered as he angrily stabbed at his salad.

"John," my mom said with a warning in her voice.

He looked at her with raised eyebrows.

"You promised to be nice. Now, either be nice or get comfortable on the couch because that's where you'll be sleeping tonight," Mom announced in a sickly sweet voice before turning to face us with a bright smile and a question, "Now, who wants dessert?"

*   *   *

Dinner ended without any more passive-aggressive comments from my dad about Archer and an apple pie that tasted way too good to be my mom's.

It was definitely store-bought.

Archer had offered to help clean up after dinner and we were currently in the kitchen loading the dishwasher.

"You ready for tomorrow?" he asked as he placed the last plate into the dishwasher.

I groaned dramatically before answering, "It can't get here fast enough."

He gave me a small smile and shook his head. "Your parents that bad, huh?"

I sighed before hopping to sit on the counter. "You don't know the half of it. Ever since the . . . incident, they have been crazy overprotective. I had to beg and plead for them to even let me go on this trip."

He came to stand between my legs before reaching up to push a stray strand of my hair behind my ear. "Can you really blame them though? Especially after what we went through?"

"No, I guess not. But they're smothering me."

"They're your parents. They were put on Earth specifically to smother you," he stated like it was a no-brainer.

"Well, your parents don't."

"You don't know that," he tried lamely to defend.

"Oh really? So did you have to beg them to let you go on this trip? Do you have to give them a rundown of your day before your day even starts? Are they considering making you miss a year out of college because they think you're not ready for it?"

I don't know why, but it was like all my frustration about the whole situation had suddenly come to the surface.

Did I think that my parents were acting the way they did just to upset me? Of course not. I knew my parents were doing what they were doing because they loved and cared about me and wanted me safe. But how would they get over it if they didn't let me live my life? I had a hard enough time as it was trying not to look over my shoulder every second and expecting some nut job to be standing behind me.

I gently pushed him back and hopped off the counter, ready to call it quits for the night and go to my room and pout like a little kid, but before I could make it to the stairs, he grabbed my wrist.

"Woah! Hey, calm down. I didn't mean to make you mad."

I sighed and turned to face him. It was not his fault my parents were being overprotective.

"I'm not mad at you. It's just . . . frustrating." I took a deep breath, calming myself down before speaking again. "Sorry for snapping at you. It's not your fault I'm about to become a hermit."

He surprised me by suddenly pulling me to his chest and wrapping his arms around me. "It'll get better. This whole thing will blow over soon, and things will go back to normal," he promised.

"I hope so," I replied quietly.

"For now, let's focus on this week. It'll be you, me, and that new bikini you just bought."

Despite my mood, I actually laughed, pulling back to look up at him. "We were having a moment. Will you quit being such a pervert?" I asked with a small, teasing smile.

He pretended to think about it for a second before he looked back at me. "Nope. You know you love my pervy ways."

"You're right. What would I ever do without you?" I asked sarcastically.

He smiled and quickly kissed my forehead.

14

"You could always buy some toys to keep you company. They wouldn't be able to compare to me, though."

It wasn't until after he had darted out of the kitchen laughing his head off that I realized what kind of toys he was talking about, and I stood there with a burning face.

I was going to kill him.

CHAPTER FOUR

After dinner and a promise from me to kill him for his earlier joke Archer left and I headed upstairs to shower.

I had just stepped out of the shower when I heard my phone blaring out "Don't Cha" by the Pussycat Dolls, but instead of the original version, it was currently blaring the lyrics, "Don't cha wish your boyfriend was hot like me?"

Long story short, Archer had gotten ahold of my phone.

I quickly wrapped myself in a towel and hurried to my room. I plopped down on my bed and answered my phone without bothering to see who was calling.

"Talk to me," I answered.

"Gemma Conners?" a raspy voice asked.

"Yes . . . who is this?" I pulled my phone away from my ear to look down at the number but did not recognize it.

When I put the phone back to my ear, there was a laugh on the other line before the voice answered, "I'm a friend of yours. I just thought I'd call to check up on you and to say I hope you have fun on your trip tomorrow. Hopefully, we'll see each other soon."

Then the line went dead.

What the hell?!

My heart was pounding as I frowned at my phone before placing it on my nightstand.

This was all I needed.

I tried to calm my racing heart. It was probably just one of the kids from school. Everyone in school already knew about the subway incident, and unfortunately some were absolutely childish, so they were probably just trying to freak me out.

Too bad it worked.

I quickly changed into my pajama shorts and a T-shirt before climbing under my covers.

As I lay there, I contemplated going and telling my parents about the phone call but eventually decided against it. If I told them, they would only freak out even more, and I would end up spending my senior trip at home. So instead, I just tried to put the phone call out of my mind and eventually fell asleep.

*   *   *

"Are you sure you have everything?" my mom asked yet again.

"Mom, I'm sure. We checked, double-checked, and then tripled-checked. I have everything."

At the moment, I was sitting in the backseat of my parent's Jeep, parked in the parking area near my departure terminal at the JFK International Airport.

I opened the car door and went to grab my suitcase from the trunk. Once I had it, I hurried to the front of the car and waited for my parents.

I was a little bummed that my little brother, Aiden, was not with us. My mom had dropped him off at my grandparents' house yesterday morning since they had been dying to see him.

"You ready?" my dad asked as he got out of the car.

I smiled and nodded. I was beyond ready.

"Alright then, let's go."

My dad offered to take my suitcase, and I let him.

Once inside the airport I instantly spotted most of my senior class, and one blonde, in particular, came rushing toward me.

17

"Gemma!" Megan squealed before crushing me into a hug.

I laughed before untangling myself from her. "It's good to see you too," I said with a smile.

"Oh my gosh, I'm so excited! Can you believe it? Hawaii! We're going to Hawaii! I've always wanted to go to Hawaii. I read once that—"

"Megan!" I called out loudly, cutting her off.

"Hmm?"

"Breathe."

Megan took a deep breath and then exhaled. "Sorry, I'm just really excited," she repeated with a huge smile.

"Well, it seems like you're all set here," Dad said.

I turned to look at him and my mom and went to give them both hugs.

"Be safe, okay?" Mom said after kissing me on the forehead.

"Mom, people are looking," I mumbled as I heard a few snickers from my class.

"Let them look. I'm savoring my last few moments with my baby before she leaves for Hawaii."

To my surprise, my mom actually had tears in her eyes.

I hugged her again. "Mom, I'm only going to be gone for a week."

"I know, but it's going to seem like forever."

I let my mom gush over me for a few more minutes until my dad finally cut in.

"Alright, Sue, that's enough. Let her go be with her friends."

My mom did not look too happy about it, but after a few more "Be safe." and a promise to call her every day, she let me go, and I joined Megan and the rest of my class.

I was talking with Megan and her boyfriend, Blake, as we waited for everyone to arrive when I suddenly felt an arm snake around my waist and pull me back against a hard chest.

18

I tilted my head up to see Archer smiling down at me.

"Hey."

"Hey."

"Really?" Megan commented.

I turned to look back at her with a frown. "What?"

"You two have been dating for what? Like six months now and that's how you greet each other? Just . . . hey? Gemma, I thought I taught you better than that. You're supposed to swallow his face."

I felt my face burn. "Megan!"

"What? You know you want to. Are you shy? Do you want me to turn around?"

I turned around and buried my face in Archer's shirt. "I need a new best friend," I mumbled into his shirt.

I felt him laugh before Megan started talking again.

"There you go, you're getting closer. Now all you have to do is reach up, and BOOM! You two have yourselves a face sandwich."

Oh. My. Goodness.

He leaned down, so his mouth was near my ear. "I say we give her what she wants. I've never been one to disappoint," he whispered, his breath fanning my ear and sending shivers through my body.

I was about to reply but the voice of Mr. Frazier, our history teacher interrupted. "Alright, everybody. Everyone is here. It's time to go check in. Make sure you have your IDs and tickets and follow me."

"Guess we'll finish this conversation later," Archer said, smiling smugly.

"Indeed," Megan said with a cheeky smile sent my way.

I groaned.

How was I going to survive a week with these two?

CHAPTER FIVE

"Would all passengers traveling to Honolulu on Flight HA 365, please have your boarding passes ready for boarding. Flight HA 365, now boarding at Gate A5." A female voice rang out over the terminal.

We were currently queueing to board when Megan said the most outrageous thing, "Do you think I should've brought a parachute?"

I gave her a blank look before asking, "Why would you bring a parachute?"

"Um, hellooo?! If the plane crashes, I can jump out." She knocked her fist on my forehead.

I swatted her hand away.

"Use that brain of yours sometimes," she said with a smirk on her face.

I simply shook my head and turned to face forward. There was no point in trying to explain anything to her. She had an answer for everything.

The silence lasted a good two seconds before she was prattling again.

"My feet are killing me. How long does it take for someone to board a plane?" Megan complained.

Because our class was so large, we had to fly in two different planes. Half of our class was on the same flight with us, our history teacher and a few chaperones. The other half was on another. They had to wait about an hour for their flight and were with our English teacher and the other chaperones. Lucky for me that I was with the group that was boarding now, and Megan, Archer, and Blake were also boarding with me. Unfortunately, so were Avery and Cade.

"Could you quit complaining? You're giving me a headache," Avery snapped from behind us.

Before I could say something to hold back Megan, she was already spinning around and was in Avery's face.

"Your entire existence gives me a headache, but do you see me complaining?" Megan snapped.

Avery's face turned a bright shade of red, and she clenched her hands into fists before taking a step forward. "Listen here, you little—"

"Babe, calm down," Cade's voice butted in as he wrapped an arm around her shoulder.

Avery glanced at him before turning back to glare at Megan.

"You better watch it. It's going to be a long week," Avery snarked before she grabbed Cade's hand and yanked him forward, shoving her boarding pass into the hands of the startled airline staff at the departure gate.

"What was that about?"

I turned to see Archer and Blake standing behind us, holding McDonald's takeout bags.

"Your ex is a complete bitch," Megan snarled before quickly snatching the bag of food out of Blake's hand.

"You better have bought my apple pie," she said before stomping to the front and handing her boarding pass to the woman at the departure gate.

I glanced at Blake, who looked completely lost. Poor Blake. It could not be easy being Megan's boyfriend. I patted him on the shoulder and gave him a sympathetic look.

21

"She'll calm down after she eats. You did buy her an apple pie, right?" I asked.

Blake nodded.

"You should be fine then."

Blake just nodded again, still looking lost, before he moved forward to let the woman check his boarding pass.

"So Megan had a run-in with Avery?" Archer asked as we were walking toward the plane.

I nodded. "Words were exchanged."

He shook his head and sighed heavily. "I'm sorry about Avery. She's been—"

"Bitchy?" I added helpfully.

Archer smirked. "I was going to say moody but bitchy works too."

I laughed and grabbed Archer's hand as we continued to the plane.

To say the plane was chaotic would have been an understatement. A few were still scrambling to stow baggage in the overhead bins as others looked for their seats, some just standing by chatting with friends whose seats were farther away. I barely had room to walk to my seat.

I checked my ticket again to see where I was supposed to sit. Seat 24A. I walked further and found my seat in the middle of the plane. I smiled to myself when I realized I had the window seat.

I quickly slid into my seat and buckled in as I waited for everyone else to settle down. I noticed Blake and Megan a few seats ahead of me and Archer was seated one row in front of me to my right near the aisle.

Apparently, today was not my day because Cade was plopping down in the seat next to me a few moments later.

I turned to glare at him. "What the hell are you doing?" I asked.

22

Cade buckled his seat belt and got himself comfortable before he looked over at me. "I'm sitting down, what does it look like?"

I rolled my eyes before crossing my arms across my chest. "I can see that. What I want to know is, why you're sitting next to me? Go find her royal bitchiness and sit with her," I snapped.

Cade raised an eyebrow. "Her royal bitchiness?"

"Avery," I deadpanned.

"Oh . . . well, as much as I'd like to sit with her, I can't. This is my seat, and the flight is already full, so it looks like you're stuck with me," Cade reasoned before turning his head away.

I groaned and leaned my head against the window.

This was just great.

After a few seconds passed, he turned back to look at me. "I think your boyfriend is trying to kill me with his eyes."

I turned toward Archer, who was glaring at Cade and gripping the armrests of his seat so tight that his knuckles were white.

I groaned again and closed my eyes.

If I were lucky, maybe I would get through this flight without Archer murdering Cade by throwing him off the plane.

CHAPTER SIX

Sitting next to Cade for twelve hours was by far the worst experience of my life, and given what I recently went through, that was saying something.

We had not even been in the air for an hour, and I was already considering jumping out of the plane.

When Cade started to try and make conversation, I almost shot out of my seat to head for the emergency exit.

"How is he?" Cade had asked out of the blue.

I was planning on ignoring him for the entire flight, but my curiosity won out, and I frowned and turned to look at him.

"Who?"

"Archer. How is he?" Cade asked like it was obvious to me.

I narrowed my eyes at him as I felt my temper flare up. "After what you did, you have no right to ask about him. Just know that he's doing a hell of a lot better without you in his life."

Cade's eyes widened in shock before he looked down in obvious guilt. "I never meant to hurt him. He's my best—"

"Was," I corrected.

Cade swallowed hard. "Right. He was my best friend. I would never do anything to hurt him intentionally."

Right, because going behind his back and banging his girlfriend meant, *I'm not doing this to hurt you.*

I folded my arms across my chest.

"Except you did."

Cade sighed heavily.

"Yeah . . . I did. But you have to understand that I didn't mean for any of it to happen. It's just that one thing led to another and—"

I held my hand up, effectively cutting him off. "I really don't give a damn. I don't want to hear your excuses or about how you ended up with Avery. She's a jackass, and you're an even bigger one. End of story."

Apparently, Cade had grown tired of me bashing his girlfriend because he clenched his hands into fists before saying anything else.

"Look, I know I was in the wrong, but you don't even know her, so stop talking about her like you do."

Funny. Archer had said something similar to me back then. And yet, look where Avery was now, still with his ex-best friend. I knew it wasn't a good idea to add fuel to the fire, but I couldn't help myself.

"Oh, really? It takes two people to cheat. I think I know Avery very well." I listed off her indiscretions with my fingers. "She's slept with at least fifteen boys with girlfriends from our class alone, and who knows how many she's slept with from our school. She ruins people's lives if you haven't already noticed. I mean, she went behind Archer's back with you, his supposed best friend. Avery isn't the girlfriend type. The sooner you realize that, the better. Hell, you might want to go around and find out if she's not banging any guy behind *your* back."

I should have stopped right there. There was no need to add salt to the wound, but I was so fed up hearing his excuses for himself and Avery. "You know, I wouldn't even be surprised if, at some point during the flight, she ends up screwing the pilot."

I saw Cade's hand move before I felt the sting of his hand against my cheek. My head rocked back and hit the window, and I had to blink a few times to clear the black spots swimming in my vision.

25

When my vision cleared, I stared at Cade in utter shock, my mouth slightly open.

He fucking hit me.

"Gemma, I—" was all Cade got out before Archer was suddenly there and slamming his fist into Cade's face.

CHAPTER SEVEN

Archer had almost beaten Cade to a bloody pulp. After the first punch, the rest was a blur.

One second, Cade was in his seat, looking horrified. The next, he was supine in the middle of the aisle, as small as it was, taking Archer's fists to his face.

Two flight attendants quickly hurried down the narrow aisle and tried to pull Archer off Cade, but at that exact moment, the plane hit turbulence.

Great.

One flight attendant fell backward, landing flat on her back and her shoe went flying while the other stumbled and fell into a passenger's lap.

The whole scene would have been hilarious if Archer wasn't still trying to commit murder. Archer held Cade by the collar of his shirt while still trying to rearrange his face.

The strange thing was that Cade didn't even try to stop him or fight back. Not that it seemed to matter to Archer anyway. Cade just lay there and took it. That's when I decided to intervene.

As soon as I unbuckled my seatbelt and stood, the plane lurched again, and I hit my head on the bottom of the carry-on compartment. I cursed under my breath before making my way over to Archer.

He had his fist pulled back, ready to deliver another blow, but I quickly wrapped both of my hands around his fist.

27

Archer whipped his head around so fast that I was surprised he didn't get whiplash. There was an almost feral look in his eyes that almost made me let him go.

Almost.

Beads of sweat covered his forehead and plastered to the sides of his face were strands of his dark hair.

I swallowed hard before I pushed his hand down. "That's enough," I implored quietly.

Archer's eyes darted to my cheek, and his body became even more rigid and facial expression even more pinched. I tightened my hands around his fist and shook my head.

"Cade!"

I had to close my eyes and take a deep breath when Avery shoved her way to the scene.

"Oh my gosh! What happened?!" she screeched before dropping to her knees, her usual position, and cradling Cade's head in her lap.

Obviously, Cade couldn't answer, and all he did was groan in pain.

Avery glared at Archer. "What did you do to him?!"

He had obviously tried to rearrange his face.

To my complete and utter joy, Archer ignored her completely.

The flight attendants were finally able to stand up, and they helped Avery get Cade to his feet and quickly ushered him to the front toward first class and the cockpit but not before sending death glares Archer's way.

I sighed heavily before I noticed something warm and wet on my hand. I glanced down at where my hands were covering Archer's fist. His knuckles were all bruised and bloody.

"Stay here," I told him before I quickly made my way to the front of the plane.

When I reached first class, I found Avery and the two flight attendants nursing Cade's face in the tiny galley.

28

Avery instantly scowled when she saw me.

"Umm . . . I need something for his hand," I said, gesturing back to where I came from.

The flight attendant understood immediately and quickly grabbed some antiseptic, white gauze, and cotton and handed them to me.

I thanked her quickly before heading back to Archer, still standing where I had left him.

I quickly grabbed his hand, ignoring the scowls from all the passengers, who had just witnessed Archer's own WWE match, and led him to the toilet at the back of the plane.

Once I had locked the door, I faced Archer. But since the space was so small, I was almost pressed against him.

I cleared my throat before I pointed to the toilet seat. "Sit."

Archer glanced at the toilet and scrunched up his nose. "I don't want to."

"There's barely any space here. Do you want to do it standing up?" I asked.

Archer raised an eyebrow. "I usually prefer to do it lying down, but if you want to do it standing up, that's fine with me."

My eyes widened before I smacked his chest. "That's not what I meant! I was talking about your hand. If you're not going to sit down, do you want me to fix it standing up?"

Archer made another face at the toilet before he leaned back against the sink. "I'll stand."

I sighed, before I set the first aid supply on the sink, and washed my hands. After drying my own hands, I gently grabbed his hands, held them over the sink, and washed them. Then I poured antiseptic on a cotton ball and dabbed his wounds. Archer winced, and I mumbled a quick sorry before finishing and wrapping it with the gauze. I did the same with his other hand before I let it go, cleaned up, and gathered the supplies.

"There. Now, as long as you don't punch anybody else in the face, you should be fine," I teased.

When I looked up, I found Archer staring at me intently.

When he lifted his hand to my face, I flinched. I hadn't meant to. I knew he would never lay a finger on me, but I just did get slapped in the face, and the entire right side of my cheek was throbbing. I could see the anger brimming in his eyes when I did, and I knew it was not at me.

"I should fucking kill him," he gritted through clenched teeth.

I sighed and shook my head. "No, you shouldn't, but I appreciate the thought. Now let's go back to our seats. I'm sure they won't mind you taking Cade's seat now."

Just mentioning Cade's name seemed to make his temper flare. So I stood on my tiptoes and kissed him quickly before opening the door, only to find the two flight attendants, who had helped Cade, standing there with disapproving looks on their faces.

Somebody was in trouble.

CHAPTER EIGHT

Lucky for Archer, all the flight attendants did was give him a stern talking-to accompanied by glares. It wasn't like they could have done much else forty-thousand feet in the air. They transferred Cade toward the front of the plane, and Archer took Cade's previous seat to avoid any more confrontations.

After everything had calmed down a bit, and Archer had assured the flight attendants that he wouldn't punch anybody else, they finally returned to their stations at the front of the plane.

As soon as they were out of earshot, Archer slumped in his seat and grumbled, "I'm going to kill him."

I turned to look at him. "I thought you said you were over it."

"I lied."

I sighed heavily. "Archer, just let it go. Please. I want us to enjoy this trip, and we can't do that if you're constantly trying to kill Cade."

"I'll kill him quickly then," he grumbled.

I stared at him for a few moments before I leaned over and kissed him on the cheek.

Archer blinked in surprise before he turned to look at me. "What was that for?" he asked with a silly grin forming on his lips.

I smiled and just shook my head. "Just for being an awesome boyfriend."

The grin on his face turned into a soft smile as he grabbed my hand and then slowly wound his fingers in my hair with the other.

When he started leaning forward, I met him halfway until his lips pressed firmly against mine.

The kiss was slow and sweet, leaving me breathless when he pulled away.

I was practically beaming.

"What was that for?" I repeated his earlier question.

"For being a perfect girlfriend."

I felt my face heat up before I turned to look out the window.

Great. We *were* turning into that couple.

"I am pretty awesome. I don't know about perfect, though."

Archer reached forward and gently turned my head, so I was looking at him again. "What would you do if I cheated on you?"

I blinked in surprise, not quite sure if I had heard him correctly. Where the hell did that come from?

"What did you say?"

"I said, what would you do if I cheated on you?" he repeated.

"Before or after your funeral?"

Archer opened his mouth to say something, but I cut him off.

"Why would you ask me something like that? Are you trying to hint at something? Have you cheated on me? I swear on my dead goldfish, Archer Daniels, if you've cheated on me, I'll castrate you and shove—"

Archer reached forward and covered my mouth with his hand.

He stared at me with that soft smile on his face again before he quietly said, "See? You're perfect."

When he took his hand away, I stared at him for a few seconds before punching him in the shoulder.

"Ow! What was that for?" Archer demanded, rubbing his shoulder.

"For asking me that stupid question! I thought you were trying to tell me you had cheated on me!"

Archer, actually, had the nerve to laugh. "I'd have to be pretty damn stupid to do something like that."

I raised my eyebrows. "And why is that? Are you scared of what I'd do to you if you did?"

"No . . . well, yes, but that's not the point. The point is that, anybody who would purposely do anything to hurt you obviously doesn't have it all upstairs. That or they're just a grade-A jackass."

I laughed before I took Archer's hand in mine.

"As corny as it sounds, as long as I have you, I'll be fine."

Archer smiled before pressing a quick kiss to my lips.

"Then you have nothing to worry about."

*   *   *

When we landed in Honolulu, it was around 8:00 PM. It would be another hour or two before the other plane arrived with the rest of the students. So after everyone had claimed their luggage, Mr. Frazier decided to take us so that we could check into our hotel.

We all loaded up on a resort bus and headed toward the hotel.

When we arrived at the hotel, I was pretty sure someone was playing a prank on us because there was no way we could afford the place the bus had dropped us off at.

The building was massive and cream-colored, surrounded by swaying palm trees. The sounds of the waves crashing against the shore signaled the ocean was nearby. The numerous massive flower arrangements inside the lobby, seen through the floor-to-ceiling transparent glass doors and walls, and the various tropical flowers dotting the ground might be the source of the scent permeating the air. The modern décor and relaxed atmosphere made everything idyllic.

It was stunning.

"Wow!" Megan exclaimed in awe.

"I know." I agreed, still eyeing the building in front of me.

"All right, everybody. Let's head inside and get you guys your assigned rooms," Mr. Frazier announced as he moved to stand in front of us.

Before anybody could move, a group of boys took off running for the front doors and calling dibs on the hot tub.

Mr. Frazier sighed and shook his head. "Will the rest of you please follow your classmates in a more civilized manner?"

As we all shuffled past, I saw what seemed like a camera flash coming from my right. I turned in the direction of the flash but all I saw were the gently swaying palm trees.

Frowning, I looked up into the sky, thinking that maybe it had been lightning, but all I saw was a clear navy sky scattered with stars.

I turned to face the palm trees again with a look of concentration.

I hadn't imagined it, had I?

"Hey, you okay?"

I jumped in fright and spun around to find Archer staring at me curiously. I glanced back over my shoulder one more time before turning back to face him.

"Ugh, yeah. I just thought I saw something."

Archer glanced over my shoulder before meeting my eyes again. "I don't see anything."

"Yeah, I think I was just seeing things," I said quickly, trying to brush it off.

Archer nodded slowly before he grabbed my hand. "Come on. Let's go catch up with everybody."

I nodded and stole one last glance behind me before I let Archer lead me inside the hotel.

CHAPTER NINE

When we first arrived, I thought the outside was stunning, but it was nothing compared to the inside of the hotel.

The first thing I noticed when we entered the lobby was the gold veins of the black marble floor that shimmered under the recessed overhead lights, wall sconces, and table lamps. All the lights made the floor almost hard to look at. A set of large white couches and armchairs that held red fluffy-looking throw pillows arranged into a square surrounding a dark wood and glass coffee table with large yellow flowers in glass vases looked ultra-modern but also comfortable and cozy. There was even a water feature in the wall made to look like a waterfall, where the water cascaded over black, white, and blue rocks before coming into the small pool at the bottom.

Megan leaned over to whisper in my ear. "I bet twenty that Mr. Frazier is secretly a drug dealer."

My eyes widened before I turned to look at her. "What?"

"Obviously, he paid for this place with his drug money. There's no other explanation." Megan gasped like something suddenly occurred to her before she grabbed my shoulders and shook me violently. "What if he's a drug lord?!" she whispered harshly.

I grabbed Megan's hands to stop her from shaking me some more before my brain became mush. "Mr. Frazier is not a drug lord. I mean, look at him."

We both turned to look at Mr. Frazier as he struggled to pull his suitcase down one of the steps leading into the lobby.

"Now, does that look like a drug lord to you?" I asked as I turned to look back at Megan.

"Never judge a book by its cover," Megan said as she narrowed her eyes in suspicion, continuing to watch Mr. Frazier.

I sighed and shook my head.

"I bet thirty to your twenty that he's actually a hired foreign sniper," Archer helpfully added.

Megan scoffed and shook her head. "No way. He's definitely a drug lord."

"Nope, he's a foreign sniper for sure. He's probably from Alpacastan," Archer stated with confidence.

"That's not even a country," I pointed out.

"Yeah, it is," Archer stated like it was obvious. "It's the motherland of all things Alpaca-related."

"You guys are ridiculous," Blake butted in.

"Finally, somebody with sense," I said with a triumphant smile.

"Obviously, Mr. Frazier is an undercover agent from England."

Obviously, I spoke too soon.

I stood there and listened to the idiots argue about Mr. Frazier's "secret identity" before I had the sudden urge to pee. I whispered to Megan that I needed to use the facilities and for her to keep an eye on my luggage.

She nodded absently.

I quickly scanned the lobby before spotting the sign pointing to the toilets and hurriedly made my way over to it. Once inside, I noticed that even the bathrooms here were fancy. I quickly made my way into a stall before my bladder exploded.

When I was finished and had just exited the stall when I heard the door slam shut. I frowned and walked to the row of sinks to wash my hands. As I reached for a paper towel to dry my hands, I noticed the neatly folded piece of paper on the countertop.

I grabbed the paper and inspected it. It looked fancy—thick snow-white embossed stationery, obviosuly provided by the hotel.

As my eyes traveled the length of the paper, I was surprised to see *Gem* written below the hotel letterhead. My heart rapidly thudded, and I unfolded the note.

It was great seeing you again, but I'd love for our next meeting to be face-to-face. What do you say?

I rushed out of the bathroom and scanned the lobby until I found my class standing near the elevator doors with Mr. Frazier.

I hurried over and Megan smiled excitedly when she saw me. "Hey! Guess who's rooming together?" she asked with a huge grin that quickly faded when she noticed my panicked expression.

"What's wrong?" sShe asked worriedly.

I opened my mouth to respond, but no words came out. So instead, I handed her the piece of paper I was clutching.

Megan stared at the piece of paper in confusion before she took it out of my hand. She quickly scanned the words on the paper before she looked back up at me, frowning.

"Where did you find this?"

It took a few moments for me to find my voice. "In the bathroom, right after I came out of the stall. I'm pretty sure I heard someone leaving. Did you see anybody?"

Megan shook her head and looked back down at the note. "Maybe it belongs to somebody else, and they dropped it. I mean, it sort of sounds like it could be a long-distance relationship type of thing, or something. You know, maybe some girl is dating a guy online or something, and they haven't met yet," Megan suggested.

For some reason, I had a hard time believing that. For one, the way the note was just sitting there. It felt like it was purposely left there . . . for me. And most importantly, it had my name, or at least my nickname, on it.

"Hey, what's going on?" Archer asked, peering over Megan's shoulder at the note in her hand.

I gave Megan a desperate look and slightly shook my head. The last thing I needed right now was Archer thinking that somebody was out to get me, even if I already thought it myself. It would just end up ruining our trip.

Megan hesitated for a moment before she turned around and sent Archer a silly grin. "I think Mr. Frazier might be cheating on his wife and has a mistress that followed him here to Hawaii."

"Really?" Archer asked, not sounding convinced at all, after sending me a curious look.

"Oh yeah, definitely! How else do you explain this?" Megan asked, waving the note in front of Archer's face.

"So first, he's a drug lord, and now he's cheating on his wife?" Blake asked as he stepped up beside Archer.

"I still think he's a drug lord, which would totally explain why he's cheating on his wife. I mean, being a drug lord is pretty shady business. It's not surprising that he'd have a lady on the side," Megan said, raising her eyebrows.

Blake sighed before wrapping an arm around Megan's waist. "I think you need to lay off TV for a while," he said teasingly.

"Shut up! Maybe you need to watch more," Megan responded before she playfully pushed him away.

Archer stepped closer to me and placed his hand on my shoulder while Megan and Blake argued over Megan's TV show choices.

"You okay? You look a little pale."

I swallowed hard before forcing a smile. "Yeah, I'm fine," I lied straight through my teeth.

"Are you sure?" Archer asked while studying my face.

I faked a small laugh before grabbing his hand and pulling him toward the elevator doors. "I'm fine. Now, come on. The sooner we go to sleep, the earlier we'll wake up and start enjoying our trip."

Archer looked like he did not believe a word I had said and wanted to say so, but he let it go anyway, and I almost sighed in relief.

I was just being paranoid. If I did not pay the note any attention, I would forget all about it by morning.

Megan was probably right. The note probably did belong to some woman who had some online relationship. A woman who coincidently was named Gem. That could be the only explanation. Right?

CHAPTER TEN

Besides the note incident, it seemed like the longer I was in the hotel the better it seemed to get.

The boys and girls had obviously been separated and wouldn't be sharing rooms. We were grouped into four per room, and sharing it with Megan and me were two other girls named Dawn and Becca.

I recalled speaking to Becca a few times throughout high school but could not bring myself to remember, no matter how hard I tried, Dawn's face, which was odd because she just seemed to draw attention.

She had shoulder-length auburn hair and stunning green eyes that I would definitely consider killing for. Becca, on the other hand had less striking features compared to Dawn, but she was still gorgeous, with brown hair and eyes to match.

"Oh my gosh, this is so exciting! Aren't you guys excited we're rooming together? It's going to be so much fun! It'll be just like a big sleepover! We can stay up and talk about cute boys and eat tons of junk food and watch Netflix all night." Becca squealed, and I mean that literally, before she quickly grabbed the room key from a stunned-looking Mr. Frazier, unlocking the door to our room and skipped inside.

Dawn shot me a sideways glance like she was trying to figure out if I had just witnessed what she had.

"That girl obviously needs to lay off all the energy drinks," Megan muttered before following Becca inside.

Dawn stared after Megan for a few seconds before blinking a few times and then followed her in.

I simply shook my head and was about to follow suit when a hand grabbed my arm, stopping me.

I turned, expecting it to be Archer but was disappointed to find Cade instead. I instantly shot him a glare and snatched my arm away.

"What do you want?" I demanded.

Cade was looking at me with those big blue eyes of his, one of which was now black. Thanks to Archer. And he kind of looked like a sad, beaten puppy which I figured was what he was aiming for.

Well, too bad for him because I had a thing for green eyes.

Cade rubbed the back of his neck nervously. "Gemma, I wanted to apologize for earlier. I don't know what happened."

"Well, I thought it was pretty obvious what happened," I murmured.

I watched as the tips of Cade's ears turned pink. Hmm.

"I'm really sorry. I didn't mean for it to happen." That seemed to be his go-to excuse every time he did something horrible. "Just . . . please don't hate me okay?" Cade pleaded, and my anger was momentarily replaced with confusion.

"Why do you care whether I hate you or not?" I asked genuinely confused.

This time it was Cade's face that turned pink.

"I-I just don't want you to think badly of me."

That ship had sailed a long time ago, buddy.

"I've never ever hit a girl in my life."

"So I was the first? I'm honored," I replied dryly.

For a second, Cade's mouth twitched like he was trying to suppress a grin, but as soon as he noticed the look I was sending his way, it vanished.

Cade cleared his throat and shoved his hands in his back pockets. "You can hit me if you want," Cade said, sounding hopeful.

I blinked and frowned at him. "What?"

"Go ahead. Hit me. I deserve a lot worse for what—"

I punched him.

"Shit!" Cade yelled and cupped his nose causing the students still waiting to get to their rooms to look over at us. "Oh, God. I can't see," Cade said, blinking furiously.

I couldn't help the small laugh that escaped.

Cade stopped and peered down at me over his hand which was still cupping his nose and gave me a small smile. "Feel better now?" he asked.

"I do actually. You should let me use your face as a punching bag more often."

Cade huffed and then proceeded to stare at me until it got awkward.

"Why are you staring at me?"

"I didn't think you'd do it."

I cocked my head to one side. "What? Hit you?"

"Yeah, I mean, I know I offered, but jeez . . . Is it bleeding?" He took his hand away and looked down at his nose cross-eyed, and I had to bite my lip to keep from laughing.

I wasn't supposed to be laughing! Cade was a woman beater.

Okay, maybe woman beater was a little excessive, but he did slap me, and I should not have been talking to him, anyway, given his past with Archer. I sighed heavily and crossed my arms.

"Look, Cade, how about we just forget the whole thing ever happened? If you don't talk about it, and I don't talk about it, then we can both just forget about it. And then we won't have a reason to talk to each other at all."

A pained expression crossed his face before quickly vanishing.

"I really am sorry, Gemma. I don't regret a lot of the things that I do, but I'll regret this for the rest of my life."

The rest of his life? That was a bit dramatic. He was laying it on pretty thick, wasn't he? Cade stared at me for a moment longer before he turned and made his way back down the hallway with the rest of the students waiting for their rooms.

I watched Cade's retreating figure for a few more moments before grabbing my suitcase and heading inside the room before closing the door quietly behind me.

What was I supposed to make of that?

"Hey, Gemma, could you come here for a second?" Megan's voice called out, bringing me from my thoughts.

I walked farther into the room where I found Megan and Dawn both standing with their backs to me.

I took a minute to appreciate the room. There were two large beds pushed against one wall. White bed linens with a couple of accent pillows in red and yellow graced the beds. A dark wooden desk and flat-screen TV were on the other wall, toward the foot of the bed. Two doors, which I assumed led to the bathroom and the closet, were on the right side of the beds. There was a small cherry wood coffee table with two matching chairs with red and yellow cushions on the other side of the beds. A nightstand between the two beds held a sharp-looking white and silver lamp that cast a soft glow around the room.

I was really liking Hawaii so far.

"What's up?" I asked curiously as I came to stand beside them.

"*That's* what's up," Megan said as she pointed to Becca who was standing a few feet away with what looked like a makeup bag clutched in her hands.

I frowned and looked back at Megan. "I don't understand. What's the problem?"

Before Megan could answer, Becca squealed again, rushed up to her, and latched onto her wrist.

44

"We're going to do makeovers, and Megan's my partner. You can do Dawn's makeup can't you, Gemma?" Becca asked with wide, excited eyes.

"Ugh—"

"Great!" Becca smiled triumphantly before dragging Megan over to a set of pillows she had set up on the floor.

As Becca and Megan passed, she leaned back.

"Get it off me!" she hissed in my ear.

I simply gave her an apologetic smile and shrugged.

There was no way I was letting Becca near my face with that much energy and a mascara brush. That was an accident just waiting to happen.

I glanced over at Dawn, who was watching Becca digging around in her makeup bag with a tiny grimace on her face.

"I'm sure if we make a run for it now, we might be able to get away," Dawn muttered quietly.

I laughed and shook my head. "As tempting as that sounds, I can't. That blonde over there is my best friend, and unfortunately, that means I can't leave her."

Dawn pouted. "That means we're stuck with the energizer bunny, then?"

"Yep." I grabbed Dawn's arm and started to pull her forward. "Now, let's get this over with."

CHAPTER ELEVEN

After sitting through at least two hours of torture with Becca, we were finally ready to call it a night.

Megan, Dawn, and Becca had already showered and were lying unconscious in their beds, and lucky for me, Becca was sharing a bed with Dawn.

We had all played rock, paper, scissors to see who got to shower first. Obviously, I lost, which was why I had not showered yet.

Grabbing my toiletry bag from my suitcase, I headed into the bathroom and locked the door before turning on the shower. I searched the cabinets underneath the double sinks for a towel but found none.

Groaning in frustration, I shut off the shower and headed back into the room. I went to the phone sitting on the nightstand intending to call the front desk to request more towels, but when I picked up the phone, I noticed the wire that should have been plugged into the wall was missing.

"You've got to be kidding me," I mumbled before replacing the receiver on the hook. This had to be at least a four-star hotel, and their phone didn't work?

I was contemplating between waiting to go down to the front desk and taking my shower in the morning, but it had been a long day, and I really wanted to wash away the flight.

I sighed, grabbing the room access card from the desk before exiting the room. I instantly realized how creepy hotels were at night, especially when no one was roaming the hallways.

I walked quickly toward the elevators and pressed the down button. I shuffled from foot to foot nervously as I waited.

Why was the elevator taking so long?

Somewhere down the hall to my left, I heard a door shut. I glanced to my left but saw nothing but empty halls. I turned back to the elevator and started violently pressing the down button as if that would make the elevator come any faster.

"Come on already," I mumbled.

There was a *ding*, and the doors slowly slid open. I rushed inside and quickly pressed the button for the lobby. Once the doors closed again, I let out a shaky breath.

As the elevator descended to the lobby, I shook my head. I was being really paranoid. Nobody was after me. Someone was probably just leaving their room to get ice or something.

I took a deep breath and let it out.

"You're going to enjoy this trip even if it kills you. There is no one after you," I said to myself.

Unfortunately, I just so happened to be saying this when the doors had opened at the lobby where a woman and her small son were waiting for the elevator.

I stepped out of the elevator. "Ugh, just giving myself a little pep talk," I said as sweetly as I could.

The woman grabbed her son's hand and rushed toward the opened door of another elevator. Before they entered, I heard the woman say to her son, "This is why you say no to drugs, Christopher."

Great. Now people think I'm a drug addict.

I shrugged and headed for the front desk, where a man with short dark hair in a white button-down and tie was standing and scribbling something on a piece of paper.

"Excuse me?"

47

The man looked up at me and gave me a small smile. "Can I help you with something miss?"

"Uhm, yes. I need some more towels for my room, please."

"No problem. Just wait right here for a minute, and I'll bring you some."

The man quickly walked from behind the desk and disappeared around a corner.

I waited until the man returned with fresh white warm towels.

"Here you go," the man said as he handed me the towels.

"Thank you."

"Is there anything else I can do for you?"

I was about to decline when I remembered what brought me down here in the first place. "Actually, there is. The phone in room 436 is broken. Could you send someone up to fix it?"

"I'll send someone up first thing in the morning," the man said while he wrote what I assumed was my room number down on a piece of paper.

"Great, thanks."

"Have a good night, miss."

"You too," I said while making my way to the elevators.

I struggled to press the button with all the towels in my arms, so I settled for awkwardly pressing it with my elbow. I had to press the button for floor number four with my hip after accidentally pressing the buttons for floors five, eight, and nine.

Once I was back on my floor, I shuffled with the towels down the hall toward my room. I had just bent down to place the towels on the floor and reach for my room key when something collided with my side knocking me to the ground.

I hit the carpeted floor with a grunt as whoever was on top of me pinned me to the ground. A scream built up in my throat but was quickly cut off as my face got pushed down into the carpet.

I started wildly kicking my legs to try and throw whoever was on top of me off.

"Grab her legs." I heard a deep muffled voice said. A few seconds later, I felt something being wrapped tightly around my legs. This could not be happening.

I struggled to lift my head off the ground before I let out a horror movie-worthy scream.

"Shit! Why didn't you gag her?" I heard whoever was on top of me hiss.

"We gotta go!"

Then the weight on my back suddenly disappeared before I heard several doors opening in the hall.

"Gemma!" Megan's voice filled the hallway first.

I struggled to sit up before I felt a pair of hands on my shoulders.

Megan helped me sit up while she looked me over nervously. "What happened? Are you okay? Who were those guys?" Megan fired off question after question.

I opened my mouth to reply, but Mr. Frazier suddenly showed up. His hair was all messed up from sleep, and his glasses sat crookedly on the bridge of his nose.

It would have been funny if I wasn't on the verge of a heart attack.

"Oh my . . . Gemma, are you alright? What happened?"

I opened my mouth but got cut off again when Archer shoved his way through the crowd of people surrounding me.

I was expecting him to ask what had happened, like Megan and Mr. Frazier, but instead, he took one look at me and dropped down next to me, and pulled me into his arms.

I instantly wrapped my arms around him and realized I was shaking.

"I'll call your parents," Mr. Frazier said as he pulled out his cell phone.

I pulled away from Archer and shook my head. "No!"

Everyone threw curious glances my way.

49

I cleared my throat nervously. "I mean, you don't have to call my parents. I'll do it myself."

Mr. Frazier eyed me curiously before he finally put his cell phone away. "What happened?" he asked again.

I looked at Megan desperately, who I assumed was the only one to actually see the guys who had tried to take me before they ran off.

"Mr. Frazier, it's kind of late. Can we talk about it in the morning? Gemma is fine now. I think what we all need is some sleep," Megan pleaded.

Mr. Frazier gave me an uncertain look. "Gemma?"

"I'm fine. Honest. I just thought I saw something and tripped over the towels," I said, nodding toward the towels scattered across the floor.

"Are you sure you're alright? If you want me to call someone, I can."

"I'm okay. Honestly. Sorry for waking everybody up."

"I knew it! You're just an attention whore," Avery said, pushing her way to the front of the crowd.

"Ms. Robinson!" Mr. Frazier said, giving her a firm look.

"Well, it's true. Ever since her little accident last year, she's been practically begging for attention. First on the plane, and now this. I wouldn't be surprised if she made the whole thing up."

"Enough, Ms. Robinson! Everybody, head back to your rooms. We have a long day tomorrow, and we all know how long you ladies take to get ready," Mr. Frazier said, looking at Megan directly.

The students mumbled as they walked back to their rooms until there were only me, Megan, Blake, Archer, Becca, Dawn, Mr. Frazier, and, surprisingly, Cade.

"If you're sure you're alright—" Mr. Frazier began.

"Mr. Frazier, you're starting to sound like my dad. I'm okay. You can go back to sleep. You look like you need it," I said with a small smile.

Mr. Frazier fixed his glasses before running a hand through his hair. "Alright then. You, kids, get some sleep."

We all watched Mr. Frazier in silence until he shut the door to his room behind him.

"Oh my gosh, Gemma. You scared me half to death!" Becca screeched before she bent down and literally pushed Archer out of the way to hug me. "I thought someone was murdering you!"

"Umm—"

Megan sighed heavily before she grabbed Becca by the arm. "Alright, Barbie, I mean Becca, I think we should all go back to sleep."

"But—"

"You don't want bags under your eyes, do you?"

Becca's eyes widened like having bags under her eyes was the worst thing imaginable.

"Okay then. Back to the room we go." Megan dragged Becca back to the room, and after sending me a look that meant I would have to explain later, she disappeared inside, soon followed by Dawn.

"Alright, well, since you aren't being murdered, I'm going back to bed," Blake stated before he ruffled my hair.

"Hey!" I slapped his hand away and patted my hair back down.

"Good night, Gemma," he said through a yawn before he retreated to his room, leaving just me, Archer, and Cade.

Talk about awkward.

"Why the hell are you still here?" Archer demanded.

Cade actually looked surprised. "I wanted to make sure she was okay," Cade said simply.

It only seemed to fuel Archer's anger.

"You wanted to make sure she was okay?" Archer scoffed in disbelief.

Archer stood up and was about to step forward, but I grabbed his hand from where I was still sitting on the ground.

"Archer, please. Not tonight."

I looked at Cade. "Cade, could you just—"

"Yeah, fine. Whatever."

Cade started to walk away, but just to push Archer's buttons, he threw over his shoulder, "Sleep tight, Gemma."

Then he disappeared inside his room.

Archer whirled around to face me. "Sleep tight? Where the hell did that come from?"

I shook my head. "He only said it to get under your skin."

Archer took a deep breath before he sat back down next to me. It was only then that I noticed he was only wearing a pair of gray sweatpants.

"Do you always sleep shirtless?" I asked.

"No, I usually sleep naked, but since I have three other guys sleeping in the same room, I can't. I wouldn't want to bruise their egos."

"Of course. We wouldn't want that."

"Don't try to distract me. What really happened out here? And don't give me that bullshit story you gave everybody else."

I sighed and placed my head in my hands. There was no point in trying to keep it from him. He already knew something had happened.

"I don't know. I went down to the lobby to get some more towels, and as I was trying to open the door, somebody just . . . attacked me. I thought I had heard somebody earlier, but I thought I was just being paranoid. I don't know how many were there, but it was more than one. And I don't know who they are or what they wanted."

I suddenly started shaking again and Archer pulled me into his arms. "It's going to be okay," he whispered softly.

"It was probably just a bunch of assholes trying to mess with you. I wouldn't be surprised if Avery was behind this."

52

"There's something else I have to tell you," I said quietly.

"What is it?"

"You remember earlier today when I came back from the bathroom, and you saw that note Meagan was holding?"

"Yeah."

"I heard somebody come into the bathroom while I was in the stall and when I came out, I found it just sitting by the sinks. I thought whoever came in the bathroom had left it, but when I took a closer look, it had my name on it. Or at least my nickname."

Archer had tensed, and drew a deep breath.

"Don't be mad."

"I'm not mad, but why didn't you tell me?"

"This is our senior trip. I didn't want to ruin it by bothering you with it. Especially when I thought I was just being paranoid."

Archer gently lifted my chin, so I was looking up at him.

"I don't care how insignificant you think it is. If you have a problem, come to me. Screw the trip. Prank or not, somebody just attacked you."

"Maybe they thought I was somebody else," I offered meekly.

Archer gave me a flat look.

"Or maybe it was like that movie *White Chicks* when they tried to kidnap them, but they were actually just male strippers."

"The thought of male strippers kidnapping my girlfriend is ten times worse."

I smiled and leaned my head against his shoulder.

"Are you sure you don't want to call anybody? Your parents? The police? SWAT?"

I laughed and shook my head. "Calling my parents is just like calling SWAT. I'll just give them panic attacks. It was probably just some boys from our class trying to be funny, you said."

Archer did not look convinced at all, but he didn't say so. "Alright. Well, if you're not going to call them, then you have to do

53

something for me," Archer said as he stood up and pulled me up after him.

"What?" I asked curiously.

Archer didn't say anything. Instead, he took the few steps over to the room I shared with Megan and the other girls and knocked.

Megan swung the door open immediately. She was obviously eavesdropping.

"Gemma is staying with me tonight."

"What? We'll get in trouble, and you already have people in your room," I tried to explain but they both ignored me.

Megan shot me a sly look and nodded. "Have fun, Gemma. I'll be waiting on your explanation when you get back." Megan waved, picked up the towels that had almost gotten me kidnapped, and took them into the room, closing the door behind her.

Archer gave me a mischievous smile before he led me down the hall to his room.

I guess he left his key inside because he knocked. A few moments later, a half asleep boy with messy blond hair and half-closed eyes opened the door.

"Get out," Archer stated simply.

The boy rubbed his eyes and yawned. "What?" he asked through a yawn.

"I said, get out. You and the rest of the guys find yourselves somewhere else to sleep tonight."

"What?" the boy asked again.

Archer sighed and let go of my hand. "I'll be right back."

Archer pushed past the boy and into the room. I could hear Archer from outside the room.

"Move your asses. My girl is outside. And she's staying with me tonight, so you need to find somewhere else to sleep."

I couldn't hear the responses of whoever else was inside the room, but I heard Archer's reply. "If you don't start moving, I'll tell everyone what happened at Chris' end-of-the-year party last year."

It seemed to work because a few seconds later, two boys came stumbling out of the room with blankets and pillows, both dressed in their boxers.

Archer followed with a pillow in his hand which he threw at the blond boy who had fallen asleep standing up at the door.

The pillow hit him in the face, and he snorted before jolting awake.

Archer grinned at the boys before grabbing my hand and pulling me inside. "Good night," he said and then closed the door in all three of their stunned faces.

"Why'd you do that?! They won't have anywhere to sleep," I asked.

"Trust me. They'll find somewhere to sleep. But you . . ."

Archer took a few slow steps toward me before caging me with his arms on either side of my head. "I'm not sure how much sleep you'll be getting tonight."

CHAPTER TWELVE

The next morning, after showering—which had completely defeated the purpose of last night—and getting dressed in a pair of blue-jean shorts, a white and black striped tank, and a pair of white flip-flops to match, I was in the bathroom brushing my teeth.

I snuck back to my room at the crack of dawn while everyone was still sleeping to avoid getting caught sleeping in the same room as Archer, and you wouldn't guess who was waiting for me as soon as I walked in.

<u>Megan.</u>

"So, did you guys do it?" she asked.

I paused to spit in the sink and wiped my mouth with a towel before I looked up at Megan, standing with her arms crossed and leaning against the door frame.

"What?"

Megan rolled her eyes at me. "Helllooo??? You and Archer. Did you guys do the dance with no pants?"

I felt heat creep up my neck. "NO!" I said defensively while vigorously shaking my head.

Megan gave me a skeptical look. "Hmm." She gave me a knowing smile.

"We didn't! Last night was strictly PG-13."

"So you're telling me that you had the whole room to yourselves for the entire night, but you didn't do anything?"

I shook my head.

Megan squinted at me. "You better not be lying to me."

"I'm not."

Megan opened her mouth to say something else, but three sharp knocks on the door interrupted her.

"Come on, ladies! The bus is waiting!" Mr. Frazier yelled from the other side.

Megan huffed, and before she pulled the door open, she plastered on a bright smile.

Mr. Frazier gave Megan a knowing look. "Why am I not surprised that you're running late, Ms. Levesque?"

Megan shrugged. "It takes time to look this good. Contrary to what Beyonce says, I don't wake up flawless."

Mr. Frazier blinked and then shook his head. "Five minutes, ladies, then the bus leaves with or without you."

Megan gave him a mock salute before he disappeared down the hall. Megan closed the door and turned back around to face me. "You ready?"

"Yeah, just let me grab my bag."

I went over to the desk to grab my bag, but Becca, who looked like she had already had three cups of coffee, was already holding it out and smiling brightly.

"Here you go!"

I gave her an uneasy smile and took my bag. "Thanks."

"You're welcome! This is going to be sooo much fun! I wonder where we're going."

Dawn shook her head, and on her way to the door, I heard her mumble, "Wherever it is, I hope we forget to bring you back."

Megan smiled and gave Dawn a thumbs-up before she pulled the door open.

We all filed out of the room and headed to the elevators, where we ran into Archer and Blake.

"You guys running late too?" Dawn asked.

Blake motioned to Archer. "It's his fault. He spent almost an hour in the bathroom fixing his hair."

57

Archer shrugged unapologetically. "I regret nothing," he said to Blake while wrapping an arm around my waist.

The doors to the elevator slid open with a *ding* before Blake could respond, and we all stepped inside.

Before the doors could close completely, a voice yelled, "Hold the door!"

Archer put his hand between the closing panels, and it slid back open to reveal Cade and Avery.

Great.

Avery scowled as she eyed everybody in the elevator. "Let's just wait for the next one," she whispered quite loudly.

Cade shook his head and grabbed Avery's hand. "We'll miss the bus then."

Avery huffed and let Cade lead her into the now fully loaded elevator.

As the doors slid close, I could feel Archer's muscles tense at Cade's proximity. I squeezed his hand and gave him a small smile.

Just as I thought we would make it to the lobby without Archer killing Cade, the elevator shuddered and stopped altogether, making everyone lose their footing.

The emergency bell in the elevator instantly came on.

"What happened?" Dawn asked as she pressed her hands to her ears to try and block out the harsh wailing of the bell.

No one had an answer, and we all watched as Cade pressed the red emergency button a few times.

Nothing.

"Are we stuck in here?!" Avery screeched.

"No, we're not stuck," Cade responded.

"Then what do you call it? Because it sure looks like we're stuck to me," Avery snapped. "Oh my gosh! We're going to die!" Avery wailed. "I told you we should've waited for the next elevator," Avery continued, glaring at Cade.

"Will you shut up!?" Arched yelled.

58

Avery threw him a look over her shoulder.

"You never had a problem with me being vocal before," she said, shooting a nasty smile my way.

It didn't take a genius to know what she was implying, but I kept reminding myself that it was in the past.

And that murder was illegal.

That was the only thing keeping me from snapping her neck in the elevator.

An angry and pained expression crossed Cade's face, but Avery either didn't see it or chose to ignore it.

World's best girlfriend right there.

I felt Archer tighten his grip on my waist like he was afraid I would suddenly move away from him after listening to Avery. I wrapped my arm around him to reassure him, and I felt him relax.

"Oh please, Avery. We all knew how vocal you could be before you even got with Archer," Megan said with a scowl.

She turned to look at Blake. "You remember that time we passed the janitor's closet?"

Blake nodded and then added, "And that time that we passed the old band room."

"And Mrs. Green's old classroom," Megan added.

Avery's face had gone beet red, and she kept opening and closing her mouth like a fish.

I loved Megan.

The elevator suddenly started moving again, and the emergency bell stopped its harsh ringing, stopping any more insults from flying.

Cade sighed in relief. "See, I told you we weren't stuck."

I watched the numbers above the elevator door descend to the letter L, but instead of stopping, it kept going until the L changed into a B. I frowned and looked at the panel with all the floor numbers. There was a keyhole beside the letter B. It meant only people with a key could access the basement.

So why were we suddenly headed to the basement?

The doors dinged and slid open to reveal a dimly lit hallway with gray walls and floors to match.

"What the hell?" Archer muttered as he eyed the hallway.

Cade pressed the L button repeatedly, but the doors did not budge. "The lobby button isn't working," Cade said what everybody already knew.

"Try the emergency button again," Dawn suggested.

Cade pressed the emergency button.

Still nothing.

Everybody was eyeing each other with worried glances.

We were stuck, and if we could not go up, then our only way out was forward.

CHAPTER THIRTEEN

"Are you sure the button won't work?" Avery asked for what I felt was the millionth time.

No one had stepped outside the elevator since we arrived in the basement. Instead, we huddled inside the cramped space, looking out at the dimly lit hallway.

"Do you want to check for yourself?"

You could hear the exasperation in Cade's voice.

Just like Avery had been asking the same question over and over, Cade had been giving her the same answer the same number of times.

Avery shoved her way over to the panel and repeatedly pressed the L button like we had not tried that twenty billion times already, and when that did not work, she started pressing random numbers for the floors.

When still nothing happened, Avery turned around with a huff. "It's not working."

I'm not positive, but I'm pretty sure I saw Cade's eye twitch. "Yeah, I know. I've only said it like a hundred times now."

Avery shot him a look before crossing her arms over her chest. "Whatever. How are we going to get out of here?"

"Mr. Frazier should notice we're gone," Megan said as she eyed the hallway.

"Yeah, unless he actually did leave without us. He did say that if we weren't outside in five minutes, the bus was leaving with or without us," I added.

"He wouldn't leave us in a hotel unsupervised," Megan said, shaking her head.

"So what do we do? Just sit here and hope that someone decides to check the basement?" Dawn asked.

"That's all we can do. Unless you want to go out there," Archer said, nodding toward the hallway.

Dawn shook her head.

Archer sighed. "So I guess we'll wait then."

*   *   *

Five minutes turned into twenty, and twenty minutes into forty. We had been stuck sitting in the elevator for almost an hour, and no one had come.

"You guys, no one is coming. If we want to get out of here, we have to find our own way out," Cade said after checking his phone again.

Seeing as he shoved it back in his pocket, it was safe to say that there was still no signal.

An involuntary shiver ran through me as a bad memory resurfaced. I felt Archer squeeze my hand, and I looked over at him.

"You alright?" he asked quietly.

I simply nodded and turned to look back out at the hallway.

"Cade's right. If we want to find a way out, we'll have to find it ourselves." Dawn spoke up from her spot in the corner of the elevator.

"Are you crazy!? We don't know our way around down here. We could get lost and then no one will ever find us. We should just stay here. Someone has to notice we're gone." Avery eyed us distastefully before adding, "Well, me, at least."

Megan scoffed.

"Whatever. You can stay here and wait all you want. As much as it pains me to say it, Cade's right. We can't just sit here and hope someone will magically come by. We've been sitting here for almost an hour already."

Cade turned to look at the rest of us. "What about you guys? What do you want to do?"

Ignoring Cade completely, Archer turned to face me. "What do you want to do? If you want to stay, we—"

Archer was cut off as "Hotel California" by the Eagles suddenly started playing through the small speaker sitting in one of the top corners of the elevator.

Everyone's heads lifted to the speaker as the song continued to play.

I gripped Archer's hand and looked back at him, my mind made up. "I want to get out of here."

Archer nodded slowly.

The song had obviously freaked Avery out too. Because she was gripping Cade's shirt like it was a lifeline.

"Let's go," she said while still eyeing the speaker.

Cade took Avery's hand and led her out into the hallway.

Dawn and Becca followed and then Megan and Blake.

Before stepping out into the hallway, Archer kissed the side of my head. "Everything is going to be fine," he said, obviously sensing my nervousness.

"I know," I said quietly, even though I didn't.

Archer led me out into the hallway where the others waited, and as soon as both of my feet touched the stone floor, there was a *ding*, and I turned around in time to watch the elevator doors slide closed.

CHAPTER FOURTEEN

As soon as the doors slid closed, Cade rushed past me and repeatedly pressed the up button for the elevator, but it was useless.

The doors did not budge.

"Shit!" Cade shouted as he slammed his fist against the door.

"I told you we should've stayed in the elevator!" Avery yelled. "If you would've listened to me, we'd be out of this stupid basement by now!"

Cade spun around, and I actually took a small step back. To get away from the murderous look on his face.

"Will you shut up?!" Cade yelled. "All you've done is complain since we got stuck. So from now on, if you aren't going to offer anything useful, keep your mouth shut!"

Everyone stood in stunned silence and watched as Avery's face turned a light shade of pink and actual tears started forming in her eyes.

Hmm. I didn't even know she could cry.

Seeing the look on Avery's face, Cade instantly deflated and took a step toward her. "Avery—" Cade began but was cut off.

"Don't." Avery spun around so no one could see her face.

Cade sighed and ran a hand down his face.

Archer cleared his throat. "Ugh . . . so since we aren't going to get out using the elevator, we might as well go forward. This can't be the only way out. There have to be emergency exits or something."

Everyone nodded in agreement but no one made any attempt to move.

"In order for us to find a way out, we actually need to move guys," Archer said after he saw that no one was moving.

Dawn swept her hand out in front of her. "Lead the way."

Archer raised an eyebrow as he looked at her. "Lead the way to where?"

"Out of here," Dawn said in a duh tone.

Archer frowned and shook his head. "What makes you think I know the way out of here?"

I watched as a blush crept over Dawn's features.

"Well, it's no secret what happened to you guys a few months ago, so I figured you should be used to stuff like this," Dawn said almost sheepishly.

Archer looked at her incredulously. "I should be used to it?"

"I didn't mean it like that, but it's just that you and Gemma are the only two who've had any experience with stuff like this."

"Yeah, except last time we were stuck in a subway tunnel with a bunch of lunatics trying to kill us, and now—" Archer swept his hand out, gesturing around us. "Now we're in the fucking basement of a five-star hotel. How does that even remotely sound like the same situation?"

Dawn's face was turning an even darker shade of pink.

I placed my hand on Archer's arm gently. "Archer, let it go. She didn't mean anything by it," I said quietly.

"Whatever," Archer mumbled before storming ahead.

"Where are you going?" I asked.

Archer turned and shot a look in Dawn's direction before looking at me. "Finding us a way out of here."

Everyone quickly followed Archer as he started walking away from the elevator. Before Dawn could follow, I grabbed her arm.

"Hey, don't mind him. He just gets upset when the whole subway incident is brought up."

Dawn nodded. "I didn't mean to upset him. I just thought—"

"I know. It's fine. Just give him time to cool off."

I gave her a reassuring smile and followed after Archer and the others.

*   *   *

It turned out the hotel basement was a lot bigger than we originally thought After only a few turns, I was pretty sure we had gotten lost.

It also didn't help that the basement was completely creepy.

The whole basement was outdated and didn't look like they had any intentions of fixing it any time soon. The white paint of the walls was peeling, while the stone floor was crumbling. The ceiling held dangling dim lamps, and the smell . . . it smelled like mothballs down here.

We passed a few doors along the way, but the longer we walked, the more scarce they became until we down bare hallways. A few times, we actually had to climb over small piles of stone where parts of the wall had either caved or got knocked down. With all the money this hotel had to be making, it didn't make much sense for them not to fix up their basement.

Wasn't this a safety hazard?!

"Are we lost?" Becca asked, glancing around nervously.

Ever since we left the elevator, she kept glancing over her shoulder like she expected to find someone following us. It made me uneasy.

66

"No, we're not lost. We're just momentarily confused about our location," Archer said as he turned left down another hallway.

"Sooo, in other words, we're lost," I said, looking around.

Archer huffed but said nothing and kept on walking.

After many more left and right turns and walking down hallways that looked exactly alike, you wouldn't guess where we ended up.

Right back where we started.

As soon as we saw the elevator doors, Dawn groaned and sank to the floor. "How are we going to get out of here?" she mumbled into her hands.

"Maybe we should try the elevator again," Becca suggested.

No one seemed anxious to try the elevator again, so I started toward the elevator. As I was about to press the button, I noticed the piece of paper taped to the doors. I plucked it off the door and read the words written messily in red marker.

After reading, my heart thumped harshly against my rib cage, my knees just gave out, and I collapsed to the floor.

"Gemma!"

I heard Archer's voice, but it sounded far away in comparison to the blood rushing in my ears.

This could not be happening. Not again. There was no way.

I felt hands gently cup my face before I looked into Archer's green eyes.

"What's wrong?" Archer asked, frantically searching my face.

I opened my mouth to reply, but nothing came out. So instead, I lifted my hand holding the piece of paper.

Archer took the paper from me, and I stared blankly ahead as he read it. He swore as he threw it down and pulled me into his arms.

"I'm not going to let anything happen to you. You're going to be fine. We're not going through this again."

"What's wrong?" Dawn had gotten up from where she sat on the floor and walked over to us.

Archer glanced at the paper. "See for yourself."

Dawn picked up the paper and read it for everybody else to hear.

"You know what they say about payback. It's a bitch, so I hope you're ready to pay up. Are you ready for round two?"

"What the hell is this?" Dawn demanded.

Cade rushed over, took the note from Dawn, and read it himself like he had to make sure what Dawn had just read was correct.

"Is this some kind of joke?" Cade asked as he read over the note a second time.

"It has to be. It's probably someone from our class or something."

I suddenly found my voice again and spoke up. "You guys are asking all the wrong questions."

Everyone turned to look at me.

"What you should be asking is, who wrote that note because whoever wrote it . . . they're still down here with us."

CHAPTER FIFTEEN

"Well, if someone's down here, they can probably help. Right?" Avery asked, eyeing the note. After everyone read it, it found its way to the floor and stayed.

Now, I, in no way, believed in the stereotype that all blondes were dumb, seeing as my best friend was blonde, and she was a freaking genius when she actually gave a crap about something. But right now, Avery fits the stereotype perfectly.

"Avery, if they left a note like that, what makes you think they'd be here trying to help us?" I asked, already exhausted with the situation.

There was no way I should be going through this again. As if once was not enough. What were the chances that I would be put through something like this again?

"We already said that it's probably just someone from our class trying to be funny, so we should just try to find whoever it is and get out of here."

I was a nanosecond away from facepalming.

Archer seemed to sense my exhaustion as he spoke up.

"Avery, if somebody left a note like that, even if it was someone from our class, do you honestly think they'd stick around right here for us to find them?" Archer spoke slowly and carefully, like Avery might miss something if he talked too fast.

Avery threw her hands up in the air.

"I don't know, and frankly, I don't care! I just want to get out of here!"

"We all do, but trying to find whoever left that note is a bad idea. If we want to get out of here, we're going to have to do it on our own," Archer said as he stood up from where he had been crouching next to me.

He held his hand out for me to take, and I did. Once I was on my feet, he protectively wrapped his arm around my waist and pulled me against his side.

"We don't know our way out of here, though," Cade said. "We'll just end up lost again and then we'll never get out of here."

"Then what do you propose we do? You want to stick around and hope whoever left that note doesn't come back?" Archer asked with an edge to his voice.

I grabbed his hand and gave it a gentle squeeze trying to silently tell him to calm down.

"If we don't know our way around, our best bet is to stay put," Cade calmly said, as if he could sense Archer's temper. He was already on thin ice.

"Well, I'll tell you what. If you and Avery want to stay here and be the welcoming party for whoever shows up *if* they show up, then go ahead, but I'm taking Gemma, and we're going to find our way out. I'll be sure to send somebody back for you." Archer seemed to consider his last sentence as he eyed Cade and Avery with a distasteful look.

"Well, I might send someone back," he corrected.

Archer didn't give them time to respond as he started leading me back down the hallway away from the elevator.

I heard footsteps behind us and turned to see that Megan, Blake, Dawn, and Becca were following us.

Cade looked as if he was stuck between deciding to follow Archer or staying put. Apparently, the first choice won out because he soon grabbed Avery's hand and started pulling her after him.

"What are you doing? I thought we were staying and waiting?" Avery whined as Cade continued to pull her forward.

"We should be, but splitting up is a bad idea."

Avery scoffed, "I don't care about splitting up from them. In fact, splitting up sounds like a great idea."

I shook my head and turned back to the front. Avery was seriously a pain in the ass.

"Excuse me?!" Avery's shrill voice rang out.

Did I say that out loud? Oops.

Archer turned to glare at Avery over his shoulder. "If you're coming, then you're going to have to keep your mouth shut."

Avery looked a little stunned and like she wanted to say something but simply nodded her head instead.

And so our journey through the creepy hotel basement began. Again.

*   *   *

Trying to navigate the hotel basement was turning out the same way it did the first time we tried. No one knew where we were or where we were going, and we just ended up getting lost.

Again.

"Okay, that's it. We need to stop."

We had just turned down another hallway that looked awfully similar to the one we had already been down when Cade decided to stop us.

"We've been down this same hallway at least three times now. We're lost, and it doesn't make sense for us to keep going if we don't know where we're going," Cade said tiredly.

"No one asked you to follow us. You could've stayed at the elevator," Archer shot back. "But since you did follow us and all you've done is complain about how we're lost, why don't you come up with a better idea to get us out of here?"

71

Cade ran a hand down his face and sighed heavily. "Look, man—" Cade began, but Archer cut him off.

"No, you look. I get that we're pretty much blind mice down here, but at least I'm trying to find us a way out of here. All you want to do is wait around and hope that somebody comes to help us. Take it from somebody who knows. No one is coming. We're on our own, and the quicker you realize that, the better."

Cade opened his mouth to respond, but I held my hand up to stop him. "Everybody, be quiet."

Everybody turned to look at me with confused expressions.

"Do you, guys, hear that?"

Everybody went deathly still as they tried to listen.

There was this faint hissing sound.

Archer nodded his head. "I hear it. Where's it coming from?"

Everybody started looking around, trying to figure out where the sound was coming from when Cade's eyes widened as he looked at something near my feet.

I looked down, and there was a small air vent in the wall, but the air vent was not the problem. The problem was the white smoky substance coming out of it.

"What the hell is that?" Dawn asked as she took a few steps back.

I tried to use my shirt to cover my nose, but it was too late. Whatever was coming out of that vent was already in the air, and we'd been breathing it in. The room suddenly started spinning, and when I tried to step forward, I lost my balance before falling to my knees.

"W-what's happening?" Becca asked as she stumbled and used the wall for support.

"It's the gas. Whatever's in it is—" Archer couldn't even finish his sentence before he stumbled forward and completely collapsed.

I tried to get to my feet, but the room seemed to spin faster, and my vision was getting blurry. I heard another thud and looked over to see Becca had collapsed too.

I tried to get to my feet a second time and managed to stand, but it only lasted for a few seconds before the room seemed to tilt on its side, or maybe it was me because the next thing I felt was the cold hard ground beneath me as I lay on my side. I could not move even if I wanted to.

My eyelids became extremely heavy, and I could barely look up as the rest of my friends collapsed one after another.

I tried to say something, but all that came out was a pitiful moan, then darkness followed.

CHAPTER SIXTEEN

I woke up to complete darkness.

At first, I thought that maybe whatever had been in that gas had caused me to go blind and instantly started to panic, but after fumbling around in my bag, which had somehow managed to stay around my shoulder, I found my cell phone.

I tapped the screen, and white light illuminated the small space around me, and my heart sank as I looked around the room. There seemed to be at least a dozen of what looked like broken hotel beds and nothing else inside the room.

Where was everybody else?

I only now realized that I was lying on one of the broken hotel beds, and as I sat up slowly, I winced at the dull pain in the back of my head.

I slowly shined the light around the rest of the room and saw a door directly across from the bed I was in, and seeing as it was the only door in there, I assumed it was my way out.

I attempted to get out of the bed, but as soon as I swung my legs over the edge, I realized I wouldn't be getting too far. My right ankle was a shackled and chained to the bottom left bedpost.

My heart started rapidly beating as panic surged through me.

Even though I knew it would not do any good, I started harshly yanking on the chain. The noise it made seemed one hundred times louder in the quiet room, and when that did not work, I went to plan B.

"Help! Somebody help me!" I screamed into the empty room.

"There's no point in screaming. No one can hear you."

I screamed at the unexpected voice and dropped my phone off the sides of the bed. I frantically searched the room for whoever had spoken, but I couldn't even see my hand in front of my face.

"W-who's there?" I tried to keep the fear out of my voice, but you could hear it clearly.

There was no response.

"Hello?" I called out.

More silence met my voice. Had I imagined the voice? I took a deep breath and tried to calm my rapidly beating heart.

I needed my cell phone. So I could see for myself if I really had imagined someone speaking.

I scooted to the edge of the bed, as far as the chain would allow, and reached down to try and feel for my phone. The elevated beds made me strain a bit just so my fingertips could brush the ground. I groped along the ground for several minutes before I finally felt my phone. I quickly grabbed it and sat up straight.

Praying I hadn't broken it when I dropped it, I tapped the screen again and sighed when the light came on. I slowly shined the light around the room but found that no one else was in here except me.

Or at least that was what I thought at first because when I shone the light toward the foot of the bed, I let loose a blood-curdling scream as I found Sheep Mask standing there and staring back at me.

*   *   *

ARCHER

75

I woke up to a throbbing pain in the back of my head.

I groaned and opened my eyes slowly, only to be met with darkness. Blinking a few times, I noticed darker shapes around me and sat up slowly from where I lay sprawled out on the cold ground. When I sat up, the throbbing pain in my head seemed to get worse, and I rubbed the back of my head as I tried to make out where I was.

I stood up and swayed on my feet for a few seconds before everything steadied. I felt around in my pockets and was relieved when I found that my phone was still there. I pulled it out, turned it on, and let the light illuminate the space around me. I was in a small room full of old curtains, sheets, rugs, and blankets. There was a door to my right, and when I went to open it, it was locked.

"Shit," I muttered.

How was I supposed to get out of here now?

I could always try breaking the door down, but whatever was in that gas had left me feeling dizzy and weak. I doubted if I could break a pencil. Let alone a door.

In this state, I would be no help to Gemma—

Gemma.

I had no idea where she was or if she was even okay. I had to find her.

I turned to the door, ready to try and kick it down even in the state I was in, but my phone vibrating in my hand stopped me. I looked down at the screen to see that I had a new text message.

It had me frowning. I had no signal since we had been down here, so how was I getting a text message now? I opened the message to see who it was from, and my heartbeat picked up when I saw it was from Gemma's number.

She had to be okay if she was texting me.

I quickly scrolled down to read the message, and as I did, it felt like my blood had suddenly turned to ice.

The message was not a text at all. It was a set of pictures.

76

The first picture was Gemma sitting chained on a bed with fear in her eyes and tears on her cheeks. I found it harder and harder to breathe properly as I continued and looked at the second picture, which showed Gemma again. But this time, somebody else was in the picture with her.

Sheep Mask.

In the picture, he had a fistful of Gemma's hair, and it seemed like he had to force her to remain still while taking the picture because she had her eyes shut tight, and she had one hand against his chest like she was trying to push him away.

The third and final picture made me tense up completely, with both fear and anger, and I almost dropped my phone when I saw it. Gemma was now lying down on the bed with her eyes closed. She was either asleep or had been knocked unconscious. I refused to think about the last option, but judging by her face, it was clear that she hadn't just fallen asleep. There was a dark bruise on her left cheek. Her left eye was swollen and a dark shade of purple. There was a small line of blood running from her nose and the corner of her mouth, and I could also see bruising in the shape of a hand around her throat.

No.

This could not be happening.

My hands were shaking so badly that I could barely read the message at the bottom of the pictures.

We have unfinished business. This is just the beginning. Better hurry. The clock is ticking.

77

CHAPTER SEVENTEEN

My heart was beating rapidly inside my chest.

Why was this happening? Why couldn't he just leave us alone?

I heard a tiny *click*, and a single light bulb hanging from the ceiling bathed the room in a dim yellow glow.

"Gemma Conners." Sheep Mask's voice was deep and muffled behind his mask, just like I remembered. "You and your little boyfriend have caused me a lot of trouble these past few months."

"What do you want?" I was surprised my voice sounded strong and confident when I felt anything but.

He slowly walked around the end of the bed to stand by my foot still chained to the bedpost.

I tried scooting back, not wanting to be anywhere near him, but I could only go so far.

Sheep Mask placed his cold hand on my left leg, and I instantly tried to jerk my leg away from his touch.

"You're not going anywhere unless I want you to," he said as he slowly ran his hand up my leg.

A shudder ran through my body as I stared wide-eyed at the hand that made its way up my leg.

Sheep Mask was now running his hand up my arm, and I squirmed and tried to move away, but there was nowhere I could go.

"I've seen the flyers around. They're offering quite a bit of money for my capture." He chuckled, his hand now around my neck.

"We're going to have to do something about that."

There was a sudden sharp stinging pain on my left cheek as he slapped me hard, and a startled scream left my lips. Then he tightened his hold around my neck.

"Why don't we take a few pictures to remember the moment?" he suggested with dark humor.

Sheep Mask snatched my phone out of my hand, and he instantly started tapping the screen before he held it up and took a picture, the flash momentarily blinding me.

"Lovely," he murmured as he looked at the picture. "Shall we take another?"

I shook my head, but of course, he ignored it completely. He grabbed the front of my shirt and yanked me forward before pulling me to his side.

Tears I hadn't even realized were falling fell from my cheeks and onto the bed.

"Why are you doing this?" My voice had lost its strength and confidence. It was now frail.

"Because I can," he stated simply before pulling me closer.

I put one hand against his chest, pushing him away before I felt a painful tug on my hair.

"Sit. Still," he said slowly, warning in his voice.

I watched him as he held my phone up to take another picture, and I shut my eyes tight before he took it.

"Now why'd you close your eyes, sweetheart?" he asked after looking at the picture.

I didn't answer. I just stared at him.

Sheep Mask tilted his head to the side as he stared at me through the holes in his mask. "Didn't you hear me ask you a question?"

I still didn't respond. I just sat still, my chest heaving from anxiety and fear. Sheep Mask continued staring at me for a few moments before he placed my phone on the bed and took a few steps forward to stand in front of me.

Almost in a blur, his hand shot out and was wrapped around my neck again, except this time he was applying pressure, and I was finding it harder and harder to breathe.

"When I ask you a question, I expect an answer."

I reached up, trying to pry his fingers from my throat as he continued cutting off my air.

Sheep Mask leaned in close to my face. "Do you understand?"

I shook my head weakly. Black dots began to swim in my vision, and I started feeling light-headed. Just when I thought I might pass out, he let go, and I was left coughing and gasping for air.

"I don't think you do, and it's my job to make sure that you do."

Sheep Mask swung his fist forward and pain exploded across my left cheek. I bit my tongue to keep from screaming out, drawing blood.

He swung again, this time hitting me in my nose, and I couldn't help the scream that ripped from my throat at the pain. I barely had time to reach up to try and shield my face when Sheep Mask was swinging his fist again, this time hitting me square in the eye.

Instead of another scream, a strangled sob left me.

"P-please! Stop!" I begged.

Pain exploded across my right cheek this time as Sheep Mask ignored my pleading for him to stop.

"Go ahead, Gemma. Scream for him."

He grabbed a handful of my hair before pulling my face to his.

"You made a mistake letting me live. A mistake that's going to cost you your life.

I spit out the blood in my mouth before glaring up at him.

"Go to hell."

Sheep Mask gave a dark, deep chuckle before he shook his head.

"I'm already there, but I'll let you in on a little secret." He leaned forward again.

"Before this is all over, I'll make sure you experience it with me."

CHAPTER EIGHTEEN

I'm not sure when, but at some point, I became unconscious as he was beating me. I wish I could have stayed that way, that way I wouldn't have to face him again because I wasn't sure how much more of this I could take.

I woke up feeling a deep throbbing pain across my entire face.

When I opened my eyes, I realized my left eye was almost completely swollen shut. With a trembling hand, I reached up and touched just under my left eye but quickly withdrew it, wincing at the pain.

Remembering who had caused this, I quickly sat up and scanned the room for him, my heart beating harshly, but it was empty.

I sighed in relief and sank back into the bed.

The relief only lasted for a second, though as another thought crossed my mind.

How was I going to get out of here?

*　　　*　　　*

ARCHER

I ran forward, shoulder first, and slammed into the door for the third time, but the door still didn't budge.

"Fuck!" I gripped my hair in frustration and started pacing. My right shoulder was throbbing, but I barely noticed it.

I had to find Gemma.

I kept checking my phone to see if there were any new messages, but nothing appeared and dread was slowly spreading through me. The longer I remained here, the longer it gave that creep to do whatever he wanted with Gemma.

That thought alone had me charging the door again.

There was an audible crack when my shoulder collided with it this time, but it still didn't open. Maybe that crack I heard was my shoulder.

I groaned in both pain and frustration.

I had promised Gemma that she would be okay. I promised her that everything would be fine. I promised her I wouldn't let anything happen to her, but I managed to break all three promises in less than an hour.

Guilt did not even begin to cover what I felt right now, but I couldn't focus on that, at least not yet.

I had to get to Gemma.

I took a deep breath before turning to face the door again.

I had to keep trying.

I took a few steps back before powering forward, bashing my shoulder into the door again. My right shoulder exploded with pain, but it was worth it because the door actually gave this time, making me stumble out of the room.

I winced as I stood up straight and grabbed my right shoulder with my left hand. I had to blink a few times to let my eyes adjust to the sudden brightness after being in the dark for so long. I looked around and was relieved that it appeared I was still in the hotel basement. Hopefully, Gemma wasn't too far away.

As soon as that thought crossed my mind, my phone vibrated in my pocket. I quickly pulled it out and saw I had another text message. I swallowed hard before I opened it.

This time there were no pictures. It was just a simple text message.

Remember, time is not on your side. The clock is ticking.

Before I could really react to the text, my phone went black, and suddenly a timer popped on the screen.

As I watched the time tick down, I barely had time to wonder how he could control my phone like this, as it only took me a second to realize the reason for the timer.

I had two hours.

Two hours to find Gemma.

*   *   *

GEMMA

I lay in that bed for what felt like hours but what was probably only minutes before I heard the door across from me open and close.

I quickly sat up, fear shooting through me as I watched Sheep Mask enter the room and slowly make his way toward me.

"Ah, I see you're awake. Have a good nap?" he asked, dark humor lacing his tone.

I glared at him as best I could with a swollen eye but said nothing.

He reached forward, and I instantly flinched and moved away from his outstretched hand. "Come on now, don't act like that," he said as he grabbed my face roughly.

A small whimper left my lips as pain enveloped my entire face.

"Does that hurt?" he asked with mock concern.

He let go of my face and reached for something in his pocket.

My eyes went wide with panic when I saw him pull out a syringe filled with a clear liquid. I watched as he took the top off the needle and held it up to the light.

"W-what is that?" I asked, not bothering to keep the fear out of my voice.

"Oh, now you can speak?" Sheep Mask said as he thumped the needle twiceo times before facing me again.

He reached forward, grabbed my neck, and pushed me onto the bed. I tried to fight him off, but it was no use. He was stronger than me, and he only tightened his grip on my neck.

I could only watch as he slowly brought the syringe closer to me and then there was a sharp sting as he plunged it into my neck. Almost immediately, I felt its effects, and I began to feel dizzy and light-headed.

"What did you do to me?" My voice sounded slurred like I had been drinking too much.

The room started spinning, and I blinked several times to try and clear it, but it only seemed to make it worse.

"You're just going to take another nap," Sheep Mask said. His voice sounded far away.

I turned to look at him and found three of him floating in my vision. My eyelids were getting extremely heavy.

Fingers gently brushed my hair back from my face, and somewhere in the back of my mind, I knew it was him touching me, but my brain was too foggy to do anything about it.

"Once you wake up, the fun will begin," he said before I lost consciousness.

CHAPTER NINETEEN

I was getting tired of constantly being knocked out. Every time I came to, I felt worse than before, and exhaustion was quickly starting to take its toll.

This time when I woke up, I had a pounding headache and the pain from when Sheep Mask tried to rearrange my face earlier. My left eye was throbbing, and all I wanted to do was dip my head in a bucket of ice.

I groaned in pain as I slowly opened my eyes. The pain in my left eye seemed to be getting worse.

I sat up slowly and glanced around. A startled gasp left my lips as I realized I was no longer in the same room. In fact, I was not in the basement at all. I wasn't even in the hotel anymore.

I was in the back of a van.

I quickly crawled over to the van doors and tried to open them but unsurprisingly they were locked. Sighing in frustration, I looked around for anything that would help me but the van was completely empty.

If this van were like most, then I could have simply crawled into the front and unlocked the doors from the inside, but this van had that part completely sealed off, so I had no idea if someone was in the front or not, and due to the lack of windows I didn't have a clue as to where I even was.

So I did what anyone would do in my situation.

I screamed for help, "Help! Somebody help me!" I started banging on the doors of the van with my fists.

"Anybody! Help! Please!"

The doors suddenly flew open, and sunlight flooded in. I had to shield my eyes with my hand from the sudden harsh light after being in the dark for so long. I squinted as I stared at the shadow standing before me.

"Quit screaming, or I'll have to knock you out again."

My heart dropped into my stomach as a cold shiver ran up my spine.

That voice. It couldn't be.

The shadow stepped closer, out of the bright sunlight, confirming my suspicion.

"Dylan," I whispered.

A lazy smirk found its way to his lips. "Nice to see you again, princess."

I couldn't bring myself to speak, so I just stared in shock at the guy before me.

"Surprised to see me?"

"Y-you . . . You're working with *him*? Why?" I asked, my voice trembling.

The smirk on Dylan's face faltered. "I don't really think that's any of your business, princess."

I shook my head. "I don't understand. After everything we went through, after everything he helped put us through, you're helping him?"

I couldn't keep my voice from rising as anger started to replace the shock. "He tried to kill us! He's a murderer, Dylan. He kills people for fun! Why . . . why would you help someone like that?"

Dylan glanced over his shoulder quickly before turning back to face me.

"I said keep your voice down unless you want to be knocked out again." Dylan took a deep breath. "And to answer your question, desperate times call for desperate measures, right?"

I frowned, not understanding what he meant.

"All of this could've been avoided, you know," Dylan said after a moment.

"What?"

Dylan gestured to me with his hand.

"This. He wants Archer, and he'll do anything to get back at him, even if that means using you. It's more than just revenge he's after. He wants to make him suffer, and he's using you to do it. If you had just come with me when I asked, we wouldn't be in this mess."

"Are you trying to say this is my fault?" I asked incredulously.

Dylan shook his head, and a dark look crossed his features.

"No, this is Archer's fault. You just had the misfortune of being with him, so you got pulled into it too."

I sighed and shook my head. "Dylan, please don't do this. Let me out, and we can call the police and find Archer and the others together. You don't have to be a part of this."

He gave me a sort of sad smile.

"I'm already a part of this, and unfortunately, you're not the only one with the people you love whose lives are on the line."

Before I could respond, Dylan stepped back and closed the van doors, locking me in again. I slumped against the side of the van and pulled my knees up to my chest before placing my head in my hands.

What was I supposed to do now?

I wasn't even in the hotel anymore. I had no clue where I was, and if I didn't know where I was, then how was anybody supposed to find me?

My bag and cell phone were gone. I assumed Sheep Mask took them or had Dylan do it when they brought me here. Now I had no way of contacting anybody.

I was on my own.

As it seemed, my chances of getting out of here were slim to none. I would be lucky if they let me live. But knowing the psycho behind all of this the way I did, I didn't think my chances were too high either.

So, I just sat there with no real hope of getting out and cried. I cried until there were no more tears to shed, and when the tears stopped falling, I just shook with silent sobs. When those stopped, too, I just curled up into a ball, exhausted.

CHAPTER TWENTY

I couldn't believe it.

Dylan. Of all people. He was the one helping this psycho.

All my friends were missing. I was currently held in the back of a van, and we were all probably going to die. I didn't think it could have gotten much worse, but obviously, I was wrong.

I had been in the back of this van for what felt like forever, but I couldn't be sure how much time had passed since there were no windows for me to look out. It was only when the doors opened again that I got a glimpse outside. The sun was still high up in the sky, so too much time couldn't have passed.

I only turned my attention away from outside and to Dylan when he held a bottle of water out to me, which I eyed suspiciously.

Catching my look, he sighed heavily. "I didn't do anything to it."

"Right, because your word means so much," I replied sarcastically.

Dylan held the bottle closer to me. "It hasn't even been opened. See? The seal is still intact."

"Like that means anything. You could've used a needle and slipped something in there."

He sighed again and rolled his eyes. "Look, if you want to sit in the back of this van and dehydrate, be my guest."

"Yeah, because sitting here not dehydrated and waiting for your stupid psychotic friend to come back and kill me is a much better option. Seems like either way it goes, I'm dead."

"Gemma, look—"

"Save it," I snapped.

"You don't understand."

"I don't really want to," I countered.

"He threatened my family!"

My eyes widened at that.

"What?"

Dylan ran a hand through his hair and sat down on the edge of the back of the van.

"He threatened to kill my family, Gemma," he repeated. "My mom and my little sister are all I have, and he said he'd kill them both if I didn't help him with this," Dylan explained. "He found me a few weeks ago on my way home from work. At first, I had no idea who he was. I thought he was just some whack job off the street, but then he started telling me stuff. Stuff that I hadn't told anyone about what had happened while we were down there. Stuff that no one could know unless they had been down there with us."

Dylan took a deep breath before he continued, "When I realized who he was, I told him I was going to call the cops, but he said that if I did, he'd not only kill me but my mom and little sister too. Then he told me what he wanted from me. He wanted me to help him with this whole crazy plan that he has to get back at Archer."

The entire time Dylan was talking, he wouldn't look at me until now, and my heart broke a little when I saw tears in his eyes.

"He told me that he'd find me again in a couple of weeks, and when he did, I had better be ready." He took another deep breath. "Gemma, you have to believe me. I didn't want to do this. I don't want to do it, but he'll kill my mom and my sister if I don't. I haven't even seen them for almost a week now. That's how long he's had me with him, and my mom and sister have no clue where I am or what happened to me, and I'm scared shitless right now."

Dylan let his head fall back against the door of the van. "I don't really like Archer. I borderline hate the guy, but I don't want him dead. I just . . . I don't know what to do. I feel like no matter what I do, someone I care about is going to pay if I don't do what he asks." He looked me right in the eye when he said this.

Probably against my better judgment, I crawled to sit next to him and placed a hand on his shoulder.

Dylan looked at me with a sad expression and then slowly lifted his hand to my face and cupped my cheek. "Look at what he's already done to you."

"Yeah, I probably don't look too great right now." I tried to smile, but it probably came across as more of a grimace.

Dylan let his hand fall from my face and then sighed heavily. "It'll be a thousand times worse if I don't do what he says."

"It doesn't have to be like this," I said quietly. "Let me go, and we can find my friends together, then we can go to the police."

"Gemma—" Dylan began tiredly, but I cut him off.

"Dylan, please. All my friends are missing, and he's probably going to kill them all if we don't do anything about it."

"Gemma, I don't have a choice. Your friends' lives aren't the only ones on the line."

"But if we could just get to the police, then you wouldn't have anything to worry about."

"That's not a chance I'm willing to take."

"He's going to kill me too, Dylan. If this whole thing is just to get back at Archer, then he'll kill me, and he'll make sure Archer knows, which means before he goes to kill Archer, he'll have to kill me first. I'm not saying my life is more important than your mom's or your sister's," I continued. "But we could probably save everybody if we could just get to the police. He obviously trusts you enough to guard me on your own. We could make a run for it and get to them, then all of this would be over."

Dylan didn't say anything. He just stared down at his hands, clenched in his lap. After a moment he got up, put the water bottle down next to me, and stepped back.

"I'm sorry, Gemma," he said before closing the doors to the van.

CHAPTER TWENTY-ONE

Even more time passed that I could not keep track of as I continued to sit in the back of this stupid van. I could have been sitting here for hours or maybe only minutes. At this point, I didn't really care. I just wanted to get out.

It was starting to get very hot inside the van. I had already thrown caution to the wind and guzzled the water Dylan had left behind, and I was still extremely thirsty.

I leaned my head back against the side of the van and had actually started to doze off when the doors were opened, yet again, only this time it wasn't Dylan there to greet me.

It was Sheep Mask.

"Hello, Gemma. How are you feeling?"

He asked me this as if we were old-time friends catching up as if he had not just tried to give me a makeover via his fist a little while ago.

"I'd be a lot better if you put your head under the tire and put the van in reverse."

Sheep Mask, obviously, was not amused by my reply.

"I'd thought you'd have learned your lesson from earlier, Gemma. Getting smart with me will only end badly for you."

"I honestly don't think it could get any worse than it is now," I said as I glared at him. "If you wanted to kill me, I think you'd have done it by now. So what exactly is it that you're waiting for?" I questioned.

"I don't think you quite understand your position here," he answered after a tense silence.

He reached forward and grabbed the front of my shirt before roughly pulling me toward him until my face was only a few inches from his.

"I'm in control here. You don't get to ask me questions. The only thing you get to do is what I allow. Understand?"

When I didn't respond, Sheep Mask clenched his fist before I felt it connect with my cheek. My face was still bruised, bloody, and sore from before, and the pain only intensified when he hit me again.

"I asked you a question. If you want to make it through the day I'd suggest you answer." Sheep Mask growled out. "I'll repeat myself one time and one time only. Do. You. Understand?"

I really did not want or need him to hit me again, so I nodded.

Sheep Mask released his grip on my shirt and patted my cheek, which made me wince. "Good girl. Now get out of the van."

I frowned and scooted back into the van. "What?"

"Did I stutter? I said get out of the van," he said slowly and I could tell his patience had already been worn out, but even so, I didn't budge.

"W-why?" My voice trembled as I stared at him. If he wanted me to get out of the van, it couldn't be because he suddenly gained a conscience and had decided to let me go.

Sheep Mask gave a humorless laugh that sent chills down my spine. "You're either hard of hearing or just plain stupid."

He reached forward again, grabbed my shirt, and forcefully tried to pull me out of the van.

"Wait, stop! What are you doing? Where are we going?" I tried to dig my heels into the bottom of the van, but he was way stronger than me, and I only ended up pissing him off because as soon as I started to resist, he backhanded me.

I could taste blood in my mouth, and black spots swam in my vision.

"Get the fuck out of the van!" he roared and this time when he tried to pull me out, I didn't even try to stop him. I couldn't, even if I wanted to.

When my feet touched the ground I realized two things.

The first was that I was standing on grass, not concrete, which led me to believe we were probably somewhere secluded. But it could not have been too far from the hotel for Sheep Mask to be able to run back and forth. A few seconds after my feet hit the ground, my knees gave out, and I collapsed to the grass.

The second thing I realized was that I was in no condition to put up a fight anymore. The sun was still high in the sky, and almost instantly, my shirt started to stick to my back with sweat.

"You and I are going to go on a little trip," Sheep Mask said, and as he bent down to grab me yet again, a sudden shadow passed across my face, and then there was a loud thump.

I watched in shock as he crumpled to the ground in a heap. When I looked up, Dylan was there holding a crowbar.

I looked between Dylan and Sheep Mask several times and then blinked a few times before I could form any words. "I thought you said you weren't going to help me."

A small smile formed on Dylan's lips as he reached out to help me up to my feet. "I guess I changed my mind."

Once I was on my feet again, I swayed for a few seconds before I felt steady enough to turn so I was facing Dylan.

"What made you change your mind?"

"You," he answered almost instantly.

"Um—

"Don't worry, that didn't require a response."

Deciding to hurry up and change the subject, I nodded my head and asked, "Where are we?"

"I think we're only a few miles from the hotel. If we hurry, we can save him."

I was just about to agree when I caught what he said. "What do you mean if we hurry we can save him?"

Dylan sighed and looked at me with a worried expression. "You know how Sheep Mask said that the whole point of this was to get back at Archer?"

I nodded.

"Well, he took you because he knew Archer wouldn't stop until he found you, which is why you're out here."

"Okay, so what about the part where you said if we hurry, we can save him?" I asked as panic started to creep through me.

Dylan took another deep breath. "When he knocked all of you guys out with that gas, he took Archer's phone and did . . . things with it before he put it back."

"Things like what, Dylan?!" I asked impatiently. Why couldn't he just spit it out already?

"I don't know how, but he set Archer's phone to explode. As in a bomb that explodes, Gemma. He told him he had two hours to find you or he'd kill you, but really those hours are just a timer for him. Once those two hours are up, the bomb in the phone is going to go off."

It felt like ice had just encased my heart. "B-but I thought he wanted to make Archer suffer and all that. A bomb isn't exactly the way to go."

"Think about it, Gemma. Archer's probably going out of his mind trying to find you before time runs out because he thinks you're going to die. When that time runs out, he'll think that he failed you, only to die himself. I don't know a better way to suffer than that," Dylan said solemnly.

"We have to go. Now. Do you know the way back to the hotel?"

Dylan nodded and held up a pair of car keys. "And our friend here," he said, gesturing toward Sheep Mask. "Was kind enough to lend us his keys."

I nodded quickly and ran to the passenger side of the van.

97

"Let's go."

CHAPTER TWENTY-TWO

I was a bundle of nerves as Dylan drove back to the hotel, breaking every traffic law known to man.

Anything less was unacceptable.

We had to find Archer in time. We didn't have a choice because I refused to think about what would happen otherwise.

I had to get to him.

"Can you go any faster?!" I demanded what was probably the hundredth time.

Dylan quickly glanced at me out of the corner of his eye, an irritated expression on his face. "I'm going as fast as I can!" he yelled for what was probably also the hundredth time.

I sighed heavily and tried to keep my shaking legs still, but as soon as they stopped, my hands started shaking instead.

I was a nervous wreck.

I saw Dylan glance at me again out of the corner of my eye and was surprised when I felt a warm hand cover both of my shaking ones.

I glanced down at Dylan's hand and then back up at him. "We're going to find him, Gemma." His voice was unusually soft.

I couldn't help the few tears that slipped out and ran down my cheeks. "But are we going to find him in time?" I asked, my voice shaky.

Dylan gently squeezed my hands. "We'll find him. Alive and in time," he promised.

I turned, so I was fully facing him. "Don't make that promise unless you can keep it."

"I plan on keeping it. We're going to get to him."

I didn't say anything in response. I just turned back forward and watched as the palm trees flew by. I watched people walking, talking, and laughing. None of them seemed to have a care in the world while mine was slowly torn apart.

$$* \qquad * \qquad *$$

ARCHER

All I had left was one hour.

I had spent the first hour searching everywhere I could for Gemma.

The problem was I had no idea where I was, where I was going, where Gemma was, or where to start looking for her.

I ran a frustrated hand through my hair. How could I have let this happen? After everything we went through, I should have known better. Now Gemma and all my friends were missing, and I only had—

I glanced down at my phone—fifty-five minutes to find her.

I felt absolutely useless. I had been searching for what felt like forever, and I was no closer to finding her than I was before. She was probably waiting for me to come and get her, and I couldn't.

What kind of piece of shit boyfriend was I?

I slammed my fist into the nearby wall.

"Fuck!"

I barely paid any attention to my now bloody knuckles. Glancing at my phone again, I took a deep breath. I was not about to stop looking for her.

I would not give up on her. Not now, not ever.

100

I was going to find her.

*   *   *

GEMMA

After what seemed like an eternity, plus some, our hotel finally came into view. What I was not expecting was the twenty-plus police cars surrounding the place.

"What do you think is going on?" Dylan asked as he slammed on the brakes and put the van in park.

"I don't know and I don't really have time to sit around and ask. I have to find Archer," I said as I jumped out of the van and started towards the front of the hotel.

I had only made it to the first police car with Dylan right on my heels when a police officer held his arm out and stopped me.

"I'm sorry, miss. This is currently the site of a kidnapping. I can't let you pass."

"Yeah, I know. I was one of the people kidnapped!"

The officer took a closer look at my battered appearance. He quickly waved over another officer—another male, probably in his late thirties, with black hair and brown eyes.

"What's going on?" the second officer asked.

"She says she was one of the kids they reported missing," Officer Hale said, as I read his name tag.

The other officer, Officer Thompson, looked at me before quickly fishing a piece of paper from his pocket. He looked down at it and his eyes went wide.

"It is her! Gemma Conners right?"

I nodded. "Yes, that's me, but I don't have time to sit here and talk right now. My friends are still down there, and my boyfriend is in danger. There's a bomb—"

"Bomb?!" Officer Hale exclaimed.

I blew out an exasperated breath. "I'll explain it to you all later, but right now, I need to get to my friends. They're in the basement of this hotel."

"Wait a minute. You mean to tell me that all the other missing kids are right in the basement?" Officer Thompson asked.

I ran a hand down my face. "Yes! If you guys would have actually looked, I'm sure you would have found them by now."

"We just found out about you guys. We wouldn't even be here if it weren't for the fact that so many of you went missing. You know you usually have to wait—"

"I don't care! " I screamed. "I told you there is a bomb, and my boyfriend needs to be found before the damn thing goes off?!"

"Miss, I'm going to have to ask you to calm down. Now that we know where the kids are, we'll find them, and everything will be fine. We'll get your boyfriend and your friends back safely," Officer Thompson said in a soothing voice.

"No, you don't get it. The man who kidnapped us is a lunatic. He runs around wearing this sheep mask, and if you don't get him, then we'll never be safe."

"Well, where is he?" Officer Hale asked.

"I don't know! We knocked him out and took off so I could get to my boyfriend in time!" I was tired of talking, so I tried to shove my way past, but Officer Thompson stopped me.

"Whoa there. You can't go back in there. Chris, go ahead and inform the chief and let them know that there's a possible bomb threat."

Officer Thompson looked down at me with a calm expression on his face. "You see? Everything is going to be just fine."

I was about to object when Dylan suddenly jumped in. "I know where I saw him last!"

Officer Thompson looked over at Dylan, noticing him for the first time. "Who?"

"The guy who kidnapped them. I know where we knocked him out. I can take you guys to it."

"Really? Well, wait right here. I'll get some guys, and you can show them."

Officer Thompson quickly turned around and hurried over to the small group of officers.

I quickly turned to Dylan.

"Dylan, we don't have time to go back and show them where we left him. Archer is running out of time!"

"I know. Which is why I'm going to show them by myself, and you're going to sneak away and find your way back into that hotel before they come back here."

Before I even knew I was doing it, I rushed forward and threw my arms around Dylan. "Thank you," I whispered.

Dylan's arm quickly went around me. "You're welcome. Now, go before they come back."

I quickly pulled away from our hug and threw him a grateful smile before quickly taking the long way around the hotel, away from all of the police officers in the front.

I was not going to wait for them to try and find Archer.

I would find him myself.

CHAPTER TWENTY-THREE

Once inside, I did a quick scan of my surroundings. There was a group of police by the front door in the lobby and another set by the elevators, which I assumed still were not working. Even though the elevator wasn't working, there was a set of stairs off to its right side, which had a white sign with a red stickman walking down a set of steps that clearly led straight into the basement.

It was not too hard to return to the basement again, which made me wonder why the police had not been able to find my friends yet.

I mean, really? Did they even look for my friends? There could have been a big flashing neon sign that said "Lost Teenagers Are Down Here," and I'm pretty sure the police still wouldn't have found them.

Cops are dumb.

I wish we could have found the stairs earlier. Maybe then, we wouldn't be in this mess now.

After making certain no one was watching me, I went down what felt like a thousand sets of stairs before I finally made it to the basement. Looking around, it looked like I was on the opposite side of where we all started off because I didn't recognize anything, and there was no elevator in sight.

This basement was a complete maze. Great.

I didn't have time to wander around and hope I would miraculously run into Archer, but what choice did I have? I took a deep breath and was about to take a leap of faith and just choose a random hallway to go down when that song started playing again. "Hotel California." I instantly froze.

I doubted that music should be playing down here. In the elevator, sure, but down here in the basement, and for it to be the exact same song that played when we first got stranded down here, it wasn't a coincidence.

That could only mean one thing.

"Gemma."

I spun around instantly and came face to face with Sheep Mask.

Well, face to mask, but you get my point.

He was holding a black cell phone, and he was breathing heavily. It made me wonder how I didn't hear him come up behind me. There was a trickle of blood running down his neck that soaked the front of his shirt. Dylan must have hit him pretty damn hard.

Too bad it didn't kill him. I guess I wasn't that lucky.

I was not about to sit here and stick around for chitchat, though. I quickly spun on my heels, ready to bolt. I had taken about three steps forward before I felt a sharp tug on my hair.

I screamed as I was yanked back into Sheep Mask's chest. I dug my nails into his hands which had a death grip on my hair, but it didn't seem to faze him.

"Let me go!" I yelled.

I tried kicking and twisting my body from side to side, but he would not budge. It only seemed to piss him off.

He turned me around quickly, so I was facing him again, and then I felt a sharp sting across my left cheek, causing my head to snap to the side.

I blinked a few times to clear the dots swimming in my vision. How many times was this bastard going to hit me today?!

"You little bitch." He sneered in my face. "You just won't listen, will you? Always have to do things the hard way."

105

He moved his hand from my hair to my throat and tightened his hand, instantly cutting off my breath. My eyes went wide in panic, and I tried clawing at his hands again, but it was no use. His grip was like iron.

He pulled my face close to his. "I should kill you right here, right now."

Go to hell, you psychotic bastard!

That was what I wanted to tell him, but I couldn't because he was literally choking the life out of me. I could barely pull air into my lungs.

Darkness started to creep into the edge of my vision, and my grip on his hands became weaker and weaker. Was this how I was going to die? Alone and in a dirty basement at the hands of some psycho?

Sheep Mask moved his face, his mouth was right next to my ear. "Killing you like this would be too easy. I have so much more in store for you, Gemma. So much more," he whispered.

He turned his head and took a deep breath.

Was he smelling my hair?!

"Would you like to know what I have planned for you?" he asked.

Like I could answer him.

"After your little boyfriend is dead, I'm going to take you with me. How do you feel about being my little pet, Gemma? Hmm?"

I tried to pull away with what little strength I had as he used his other hand to stroke my hair. He pulled his mouth away from my ear, leaning back to look at me through his mask. Although I couldn't see his eyes, I could just picture him looking me up and down.

"I can picture it now. All the fun you and I are going to have." He gave a dark chuckle. "There won't be anybody there to hear your screams. No friends, no Archer. Just me. What do you think about that?"

"I think you have two seconds to get your hands off her before I fucking kill you."

Sheep Mask instantly loosened his grip on my neck but didn't release his grip on me. I started coughing as I tried to take in lungfuls of air.

I was able to turn my head just enough to see Archer standing at the end of the hall. His fists clenched, and a deadly expression on his face.

I felt that familiar burn in my eyes as tears started to form.

He was alright.

The reality of our situation came crashing back as I eyed the phone clutched in his right hand.

The bomb!

I tried opening my mouth to warn him, but Sheep Mask spoke first.

"I'm so glad you're here. It makes what's about to happen so much sweeter."

CHAPTER TWENTY-FOUR

Archer's gaze never left mine.

I watched as he took in my appearance. The pain that reflected on his face let me know I didn't look too good. I didn't care how I looked right now, though. All I wanted was to run to him, and to get the hell out of here.

How much time did we have left before the bomb went off?

By the way he was still holding the phone, I knew he had no idea what he was really clutching so tightly. I opened my mouth to try and warn him again but Sheep Mask quickly placed his hand over my mouth.

"I don't want you to spoil the surprise now, darling," he whispered in my ear.

I tried moving away from him but he only tightened his grip and pulled me closer to him. "You're not going anywhere," he said. His mouth pressed against my ear.

"Let her go."

Sheep Mask looked up at Archer and chuckled darkly. "You're in no position to give orders."

Archer shook his head and continued to glare at Sheep Mask. "I played your little game. You said I had two hours to find her, and I did. Now let her go."

Sheep Mask laughed darkly again. "Did you really think it was going to be that easy?" Sheep Mask shook his head before continuing, "Did you actually think that I'd let you have her?"

He ran a hand up my arm, causing shivers to run through my body. "We've been having so much together. I think I'll keep her."

"Like hell you will." Archer took a step forward, but Sheep Mask quickly used his free hand to hold up a phone.

"Ah, ah, ah. I wouldn't come too close if I were you."

Archer stopped in his tracks and eyed the phone cautiously. "What did you do?"

"Wouldn't you like to know?"

Although I couldn't see his face, I could practically feel him grinning like a maniac.

"Now, here's what's going to happen," Sheep Mask began. "I'm going to take Gemma, and we're leaving. I'm sure you're aware your other little friends are still down here."

I watched as he quickly typed something into his phone and then looked back up at Archer. Archer's phone beeped, and for one horrible moment, I thought the bomb was about to go off, but nothing happened.

Archer looked down at his phone and frowned. "What is this?"

"That's the location where your friends are locked away."

Archer narrowed his eyes at him. "Why would you tell me where they are?"

"Consider it a parting gift."

"A parting gift?" Archer repeated.

"Yes, a parting gift. As I said, Gemma will be coming with me, so you should go ahead and go get your friends."

"And what makes you think I'll let you take her anywhere?" Archer asked with a scowl.

"Because you don't have a choice." Sheep Mask looked down at his phone and clicked his tongue. "You have about fifteen minutes before a toxic gas will be released into the room they're being held. If they breathe it in, they'll be dead within minutes. So if I were you, I'd get a move on."

I shook my head vigorously, trying to tell Archer with my eyes not to do it. I tried speaking again, and I even tried to bite his hand, but Sheep Mask just pressed his hand against my mouth harder, so only muffled sounds came out. He slowly started to back away with me still in his grasp.

"Tick tock."

Archer looked down at his phone and then back at me. There was a look of wild panic in his eyes.

He didn't know what to do.

If he tried to save me, all our friends would surely die, and if he went after them then I would be stuck with Sheep Mask, and who knows what would happen to me.

What Archer didn't know, though, and what I desperately wanted to tell him, was that the bomb in his phone was going to explode at any moment. Even if he got to our friends, if that bomb went off, they would all be gone.

Somehow, I believed that was Sheep Mask's intention anyway.

Tears started rolling down my cheeks as Sheep Mask backed away even farther with me. Archer took a step forward like he wanted to follow, but Sheep Mask held his phone up again.

"Time is running out, Archer. Are you really going to let all your friends die? Don't worry about, Gemma. I'll take good care of her."

I tried fighting against his grip again. This can't be happening. It can't end like this. I screamed against his hand as he pulled me toward a set of stairs. I looked back at Archer with tears blurring my vision.

He looked so torn, pain clearly etched onto his face. He probably thought I wanted him to save me. If only he knew I was trying to get free so that I could save him.

110

Sheep Mask was at the bottom of the steps with me now. I was kicking, scratching, twisting my body, anything I could to try and free myself from his grasp, but nothing worked. He kept his hand tightly clamped over my mouth and kept me tight against him.

"Well, I'd say it's been a pleasure, but it hasn't." Sheep Mask sneered. "I'm sure we won't cross paths again after this." He let loose such a dark laugh that goosebumps rose on my arms.

"Goodbye, Archer."

And just like that, Sheep Mask dragged me up the stairs.

CHAPTER TWENTY-FIVE

ARCHER

This could not be happening.

I ran my hands through my hair in frustration.

I just stood there and watched as my girlfriend got dragged off by that psycho. What was I supposed to do now? Choose between my friends and my girlfriend? How could I make a decision like that?

I couldn't do it.

Either way, someone I cared about would get hurt. I didn't even have time to think about what I wanted to do. In less than two minutes, my friends would be dead if I didn't do something.

Glancing back and forth between the darkened staircase and the hallway, I sighed heavily.

I had to make a decision, and I had to do it now.

* * *

GEMMA

I couldn't believe this.

Archer, Megan, Blake, everyone was as good as dead now.

If only I had been able to find Archer sooner.

Sheep Mask's voice interrupted my horrible thoughts.

"Don't worry, princess. I'm not a complete monster. The only one who is going to die is that horrid boyfriend of yours. I'm feeling merciful. I will spare the lives of your friends."

I continued to struggle against him as he continued to drag me up the stairs. "Go to hell," I spat.

Sheep Mask chuckled darkly in my ear. "Don't worry. Remember what I promised you earlier? We'll be there soon."

Once we reached the top of the stairs, Sheep Mask shuffled behind me before I felt the cold sting of metal pressed against my throat.

He was once again in my ear. "Now, this is how this is going to go. Once we step outside, I'm going to lead you to a van. You make a sound, and I'll slit your throat. Do you understand?"

I nodded numbly.

"Good girl. Now, let's go." He pushed open the emergency exit, and I was slightly disappointed that no alarm went off.

Once we stepped outside, I realized we were in the back of the hotel. I noticed a black police van sitting parked not too far away.

Sheep Mask started shoving me as we quickly made our way over to the van.

I was surprised that there were no police back here. Did they just figure that criminals only used the front door? Did they really not expect this nutcase to use a back door? That was literally a criminal's primary getaway.

Like I said, the police were stupid.

Once we made it to the van, he opened the back doors using his free hand. I had to bite my tongue to keep from screaming. Sitting in the back of the van were two bloody and obviously dead police officers.

Sheep Mask chuckled again. "Oops. I must have forgotten I left these two back here." He shook his head in amusement before shoving me forward. "Get in."

I turned to look back at him with wide eyes. "W-what?"

113

He couldn't expect me to actually get in a van with two dead bodies.

Another rough shove to my back told me otherwise, "I said get in."

From the tone of his voice, I knew he wouldn't be telling me again without consequences. I bit my bottom lip hard enough to draw blood as I slowly climbed into the van, trying not to step on the bodies. Once inside, I almost gagged at the overpowering smell of blood.

He ignored me completely as he grabbed the two officers and dragged them out of the van, leaving behind a trail of blood smeared across the floor.

I watched as he haphazardly tossed them to the ground as if they were nothing and then looked back up at me. "Are you ready to go, sweetheart?"

I didn't even bother answering him. This was just some sick game to him, and he anticipated seeing my reactions. I just curled up in the corner of the van and glared at him.

Sheep Mask tilted his head to the side as he stared at me. "So you aren't going to answer me.

I remained quiet.

Sheep Mask shook his head. "That's fine. I'm sure you'll have lots to say in—" He glanced down at his wristwatch before looking back up at me. "Three, two, one."

I frowned as I wondered what he was talking about when all of a sudden, a roaring *boom* shook the entire van, throwing me to the side.

Horror washed through me as if I was doused with freezing water. I watched with wide eyes as the bottom windows of the hotel completely blew out, causing the glass to rain down everywhere.

Smoke soon followed and then I could hear the screams. I could also see the faint glow of what looked like the beginning of a fire.

The bomb had gone off.

Sheep Mask cocked his head to the side and chuckled. "Well, would you look at that? I guess the bomb worked."

Before I could even respond, he had closed the door, leaving me in darkness. After that, all I could do was lean my head against the side of the van and gently place my hand on it.

"Archer," I whispered in horror and then I felt the van start up.

Silent tears started to fall, and I felt a sob building up, begging to be released from my throat as the van moved forward, and once again I was taken away.

CHAPTER TWENTY-SIX

I had no idea where he was taking me, and at this point, I didn't care either. Archer was most likely dead, and for all I knew, all my friends were dead too. I couldn't trust that Sheep Mask would just let them go out of the kindness of his heart.

The realization that I would probably never see any of them again brought a fresh wave of tears to my eyes, and I bit down on my bottom lip, hard, to keep from sobbing.

I would not give that bastard the satisfaction of hearing me mourn over my friends that he killed. The pain and anger that I felt were almost crippling. I wanted to curl up in a ball and cry until I couldn't cry anymore.

I hated him. God, I hated him so much.

As I stared blankly ahead of me at the wall of the van, tears silently streaming down my cheeks, I knew that was what would keep me going. This all-consuming hatred slowy taking over would keep me going until I killed him. Or he killed me, whichever happened first.

Either way, one of us was not making it out of this alive. I was certain of it, and if I had to die trying, then so be it.

*   *   *

At some point, I dozed off.

It felt like we had been driving for hours, and eventually, my exhaustion would not let me keep my eyes open any longer. I was not sure how long I had been asleep, but when I slowly pried my eyes open again, I realized that the van was no longer moving. I pressed my ear against the side of the van and tried to listen for anything that would give me a clue as to where I was, but all I heard was complete and utter silence.

The door was suddenly thrown open, and I almost tumbled out.

I quickly scooted away from the looming figure in front of me before I felt gloved hands roughly grab my ankles.

"And where do you think you're going?" Sheep Mask asked as he dragged me out of the van.

It was night now, and my stomach dropped when I realized we seemed to be literally in the middle of nowhere with nothing but trees surrounding us.

As soon as my feet touched the ground, I immediately slammed my head back against his face. I heard him curse loudly behind me before I sprinted forward with absolutely no clue as to where I was going.

Before I could take more than maybe six steps, I was tackled and landed face-first into the dirt. The air was completely knocked out of me, but that didn't stop me. If he wanted to kill me, he would have to work harder.

"You little bitch! I think you broke my fucking nose!" Sheep Mask hissed in my ear as he put all his weight down on my back. "But if that's how you want to play, then fine."

Hands were suddenly around my nose and mouth, cutting off my air.

My eyes widened as I tried to throw him off my back with no luck. With no options, I did what anybody would do in my situation. I bit his finger.

Sheep Mask yelled above me before he quickly removed his hands from my nose and mouth. I barely had any time to breathe before I was flipped onto my back and took a stinging slap to my face.

"You never learn, do you? "Sheep Mask asked as he stared down at me, his hands now wrapped around my neck. "That's alright. Before it's all over, you'll learn your place and be a good little girl."

"Go to hell, you sick bastard," I said through gritted teeth.

He gave a dark chuckle before I felt a sharp pinch in my right arm.

My vision slowly became blurry as dots started swimming in the corner of my vision.

"W-what did you d-do to me?" My tongue suddenly felt heavy inside my mouth.

"I just gave you something that will make you a little more . . . cooperative."

My head felt heavy now too, and I couldn't help as it lolled to the side. I felt him lifting me into his arms, and I couldn't do anything to try and fight it. I tried opening my mouth to speak again, but all that came out was a strangled moan.

My body started swaying as he began to walk.

"Don't worry, sweetheart. It'll all be over soon."

That was the last thing I heard from Sheep Mask before I could no longer keep my eyes open and simply passed out.

*   *   *

SHEEP MASK

I should have killed her.

God, I should have killed her a long fucking time ago.

It was alright, though. With her little shithead boyfriend and friends out of the way, she was mine now.

All mine to do with as I pleased.

I slowly looked up and watched as my reflection smiled back in the dirty, cracked mirror. I tilted my head slightly to the side and gave a harsh laugh.

She did break my damn nose, but that was alright too. I would make her beg for death before I was done with her. Because when I was finished with her she would regret everything.

I grabbed my mask from the edge of the old sink and put it back on my face.

Now the fun could begin.

CHAPTER TWENTY-SEVEN

DYLAN

Officer Useless had just gathered some more of his men so that I could take them to where that nut case was hopefully still lying unconscious, while Gemma snuck in and went to find Archer.

As much as I hated the guy, I did hope she found him in time. I wasn't that messed up in the head that I would wish death on him.

About ten minutes had passed, and I nearly put a hole in the ground with my pacing when Officer Useless finally came back with five other men.

Noticing that we were obviously one person short, he frowned and looked around. "Where's your friend?"

I shrugged.

"Am I her babysitter?"

Officer Useless narrowed his eyes at my remark. "Listen, kid—"

"Sorry, but we really don't have time for this. The more time we spend here talking the more time that psycho has to wake up. So let's go."

I had just taken a step toward the van, prepared to completely ignore anything else Officer Useless had to say when what sounded like a fucking volcanic explosion erupted behind me and I was instantly knocked off my feet from the blast.

I landed flat on my stomach. The air knocked completely out of me as it left my lungs in one exhale.

Wheezing and ears ringing, I rolled over to my back in time to see the remaining pieces of glass from the hotel's first-floor windows hit the ground as smoke and flames rose from the openings.

Somewhere in the background, I heard screaming and shouting, officers yelling orders, but I could barely concentrate. All that was on my mind as I watched the smoke become thicker and the flames larger and brighter was that the bomb had gone off.

The bomb had gone off, and neither Gemma nor Archer was anywhere to be seen.

I quickly scrambled to my feet, ignoring the stinging from my hands and knees after the fall, and rushed forward. I wasn't exactly sure what my intent was because I wasn't the human fucking torch, but I was stopped before I even made it halfway.

Officer Useless was looking at me like I was crazy.

"Kid, are you crazy?!" he yelled down into my face, confirming my thoughts. "The whole damn building just exploded! You need to stay back."

I shook my head and tried to step around him, but he didn't budge. "My friends are in there. I have to—"

"You don't have to do anything but stay back and let us do our jobs," Officer Useless firmly stated. "Now, you stay here. Understand?"

I exhaled heavily and nodded once.

Officer Useless looked at me for a few more seconds, scanning my face suspiciously before he turned around and quickly headed toward the wreckage.

That was his mistake.

Like hell, I would just sit here and watch. I knew what putting all your faith and waiting on the police led to. Checking to make sure no one was paying me any attention, I snuck off to the side of the building in the same direction Gemma went.

As I made my way along the side of the building, I came to an emergency exit, but any small hope I had of making it into the building shattered as I saw smoke billowing up from the slightly open door.

I cursed under my breath, trying to think of another way to try and get into the building when I suddenly spotted a white van speeding down the back road behind the hotel.

Dread suddenly overtook me as I watched the van speed away.

I took a step forward, not exactly sure what I intended to do since I was on foot. Could Gemma—

"We've got survivors!"

I whipped around as I heard a police officer shout from the front.

Survivors. Maybe they had made it out okay.

I rushed back towards the front of the hotel and quickly scanned the crowd when I spotted a larger group of policemen crowded around in a circle.

I shoved my way through and quickly scanned the faces in front of me.

Some blonde chick was staring daggers at a dark-haired boy while another blonde was clinging to his arm and was crying hysterically. A second guy had his hand on the first girl's shoulder. It looked like it was there to keep her from pouncing if the look in her eyes was anything to go by.

Standing a little off to the side was a group of girls. One with dark brown hair who looked like she was a few seconds away from bursting into tears herself, and another with auburn-colored hair who looked like she was trying to put up a strong front, but from the tremors in her hands that she balled into fists, she was scared shitless.

I knew those tremors all too well.

I scanned over the faces—first, second, third—and after the fourth time, I was sure.

Two faces weren't there.

$*$　　$*$　　$*$

GEMMA

I wanted to die. Death would be a blessing at this point.

If I thought that Sheep Mask was sick before, he was slowly showing me what a real monster he could be now. Each time he returned to the room he held me in, he left with more of my blood on his hands.

I wasn't sure how much more I could take.

I would pass out after each time he beat me, and I prayed I would never wake up again, but I was sadly brought back to my nightmarish reality every time I opened my eyes to the sight of him standing over me.

I wasn't sure how long I had been out this time, but I had just opened my eyes again when I heard the telltale sound of the door creaking open, meaning Sheep Mask was about to enter.

Just like every other time he entered the room, my heart raced in fear, and my body drenched in a cold sweat.

There were slow footsteps, and suddenly he was in my face.

"Well, look who's finally awake. I thought I might have actually killed you this time."

He reached out, roughly grabbed my chin, and tilted my face towards him. "How's my Sleeping Beauty feeling, hm?"

I used what little energy I had left to glare up at him. I had lost the energy to speak hours ago. Or maybe it was days. I didn't know how long I had been here.

Sheep Mask made a clicking sound with his tongue.

"Not talking, are we?" He cocked his head to the side. "That's alright. I'll get you screaming again soon enough."

As his physical abuse repeated, I found myself receding into my mind. Somewhere I could recognize and feel the pain he

123

was inflicting, but as if from a distance. I could hear myself screaming, but I wanted to ignore it.

I wanted to stay in this dark place I was slowly sinking into.

I was almost totally submerged in the darkness. Completely willing to let it engulf me if it meant I could escape this hell that had become my reality when I heard a voice.

"Don't."

Confusion quickly followed the voice. That was not my voice. Was I really starting to lose it?

"Don't."

There it was again. That voice.

There was something familiar about it, but the darkness was making me feel numb, and it was becoming harder and harder to think, let alone concentrate. If I could just let it take me I—

"Don't!"

The voice once again seemed to bounce around inside my head. It was more insistent now. "Don't you dare give up on me."

Who—

"You're stronger than this. You keep fighting."

That voice, it couldn't be—

"You fight until I get to you. You understand? You hold on until I get to you."

Archer! That's whose voice it was.

"Promise me. Promise me you'll keep fighting."

The darkness I had been so adamant about letting myself drown in a few seconds ago was now suddenly my enemy.

I would keep fighting.

I had to.

At least until he got to me, I had to.

Somewhere in my hazy fragile state, I heard another voice.

"I promise."

My voice!

CHAPTER TWENTY-EIGHT

ARCHER

I felt horrible.

But I had made my choice the moment I watched that bastard drag Gemma up those stairs.

I was going to go after her.

I kept telling myself that there was no way I would have been able to find everyone else in time anyway. Or at least that was the excuse I kept telling myself. In reality, had they been right there, in front of me, and I had the choice, I still would have chosen Gemma.

To be honest, no one in that group meant more to me than Gemma. That was why making my decision had taken only a split second.

It was also what made me feel awful. They were all probably dead, and it felt like it was somewhat my fault. What if I could have found them in time and got them all out?

I instantly shook my head. There was no use in thinking about it now. All it would succeed in doing was slowing me down, and I couldn't afford to be slow.

Not now. Not when Gemma was with him.

I had made it up the steps they had taken a few minutes earlier and few yards in front of me, there was a large clearing that ended at the edge of a large forest.

I looked around the clearing, searching for any sign of where that psychotic asshole had taken Gemma as they couldn't have gone too far so quickly, when I spotted a white van by the edge of the tree line.

I could see the exhaust coming out the tailpipe, and the backlights were on, letting me know it was running.

Without wasting any more time, I headed for the van.

I had just reached the end of the clearing, a few feet from the van, when a loud explosion sounded behind me, and I was instantly knocked off my feet. It propelled me forward and I landed face-first in the grass, stray branches and stones digging into my palms and face.

Ears ringing, I rolled onto my back with a grunt before I carefully propped myself up on my elbows. My heart instantly dropped into my stomach as I watched the hotel I was in only moments before, go up in a cloud of dark smoke and flames.

I only had a few seconds to make sense of the sight before me before a different sound caught my attention.

The van!

I watched as it immediately accelerated and took off down the edge of the clearing before hooking a sharp left and disappearing down a trail straight into the forest, leaving only a cloud of dust in its wake.

I quickly clambered to my feet and had to use a nearby tree for support as the world seemed to spin and tilt on its axis. I only allowed myself a few seconds to catch my breath and for the world to stop spinning so fast before I straightened and followed the van before I lost it completely.

Time wasn't on my side right now.

I had just closed about half the distance between me and the trail the van had sped down when the faint sound of police sirens sounded over the cacophonies of fire blazing, people shouting, and other unknown sounds.

Turning to my right, I could just make out the ends of a parade of police cars and the blue and red flashing lights from where I stood behind the building. Someone had finally called the police!

I hesitated. Did I chance trying to get help from the police? They were better equipped to deal with situations like this, hell it was their job, but if I went to them for help, there was no doubt they would keep me from trying to find Gemma myself, and there was no way I was going to sit back and wait for somebody else to try and find her.

By the time they found her, if they found her, it might be too late.

I took one last look at the flashing lights before continuing on.

If Gemma was going to get out of this alive, I had to be the one to do it. If he knew the police were on his tail, it might make that bastard do something drastic, and that wasn't a risk I was willing to take. Not with Gemma's life at stake.

I glanced in the direction of the police one more time before trudging forward again. I made it to the path the van had sped down. I could still see dirt and dust floating in the air from where the van had disturbed the ground as it sped away.

I allowed myself to look back before I started forward again.

I didn't have the luxury to second-guess myself. I couldn't go back on any decision I made.

Every decision I made from this point on was the difference between life and death. A game I was all too familiar with but hated playing.

I prayed I had made the right decision.

*   *   *

Hours.

It felt like I had been wandering around these damn God-forsaken woods for hours.

I was pretty sure I had lost the van's trail a mile back, when the track had disappeared. He had gone off the trail with Gemma, and I was no closer to finding her than I was when I started.

One would think there would be some kind of clue as to the way they went when a big-ass van came hurtling through a forest otherwise untouched by humans. Flattened grass, bird flying away, scattering animals.

Something. There was nothing.

The fact that it was untouched by humans was actually what caused me problems. Everything was so overgrown and dense that I couldn't see too far ahead of me.

Which brought on the question, how the hell did he maneuver a big-ass van through here? There was no way.

Frowning, I glanced over my shoulder and looked back the way I had come.

Unless . . . Spinning around fast enough to give myself whiplash, I sprinted back the way I had come.

I must have missed something. I had to have missed something.

There was no way he could get a van through a forest as dense as this one, which meant he had to have stopped somewhere before he got here, and somehow . . . somehow, I missed it.

I picked up my pace and ran as fast as I could back to where the trail had first ended. Branches slapping and scratching me across the face.

Once I reached the trail's end, I turned in a circle, looking for anything that appeared out of place. My eyes couldn't move fast enough. There had to be something here.

Out of breath and panting, I slowed my spinning and willed myself to do this slowly. I wasn't going to find anything wildly looking like this.

I allowed myself five seconds to close my eyes and take a deep breath.

Focus.

When I opened my eyes, I slowly took in everything around me. The trees with thick moss-covered trunks towered above me. The forest floor was covered in dirt and fallen dead leaves and branches.

The squirrel floating to my right . . .

The-The . . . squirrel that was floating?!

I snapped my attention back to the squirrel, trying to make out exactly what the hell it was that I was seeing right now.

I took a step closer and squinted.

No, it wasn't floating. It was sitting on top of something. A very large something.

I wasn't losing my mind after all.

At first glance, you'd think it was just a large pile of fallen leaves and sticks that maybe someone had pushed to the side to clear the trail and had built up over time. But to me, this was like finding a needle in a haystack.

The placement of the leaves and sticks, strewn together to appear random, but none of it looked natural. I took a step forward and then another until I was right in front of it. Reaching forward, I slowly grabbed a leaf and tugged.

I watched—my heart in my throat, beating loudly in my ears—as the leaf in my hand, the leaf next to it, and the branch above it all moved together.

It was camouflage netting!

Like the kind one saw snipers in action movies hide underneath, right before they put a fucking bullet in your head.

Grabbing it with both hands, I took a few steps backward and yanked until the netting fell away to reveal what I had been searching so desperately for.

I stood there for a moment and stared at the dirty old van. It looked exactly like what parents warned their kids to stay away from—tinted windows, old, no license plate—to avoid being kidnapped.

All I needed now was a creepy old guy to pop out and say, *"Hey, little guy. Want some candy?"*

If only some creepy kidnapping pedophile were my issue right now.

I glanced at the double doors at the back of the van. I had much bigger problems to deal with.

It was probably wishful thinking. He had probably taken Gemma with him.

But what if he hadn't? Holding my breath, I counted to three in my head.

One . . . Two . . . Three!

I flung the doors open, and although I knew what I would find, my stomach still dropped in disappointment. Gemma was nowhere in sight.

Slamming the doors in frustration, I stepped back and took in my surroundings. Even if she wasn't in the back of this van, she had to be somewhere around here if he hid the van here.

They weren't anywhere to be seen behind or in front of me after the trail ended since the van was here, and the forest got too thick up ahead after the trail ended.

Which meant going left or right were my only two options.

There was no real logic to my choice other than because I found the van on the right, so I chose to go in that direction too. I made my way through the trees, stepping over fallen logs, stomping through dead leaves, and scaring the occasional squirrel or rabbit.

After about fifteen minutes of mindless wandering with no real clue as to where I was going, almost convinced that I had picked the wrong way, I saw it. Sitting a few feet away, down a little slope where the trees thinned out, was an old derelict-looking cabin that looked like it had been abandoned for years.

Covering the glass of the front windows was a film of dust so thick I could see it even from where I stood. One window, busted and broken, looked like it had taken a brick or a branch. Only a few jagged shards were left hanging from the frame.

The steps leading up to the small wrap-around porch looked as if, if you tried to put the weight of just one foot on them, it would go right through. The bottom step was even missing. The wooden railing surrounding the wrap-around porch was also nothing but damp, rotting wood at this point.

It looked like the cabin version of Charlie's house from *Charlie and the Chocolate Factory*.

Honestly, the whole place looked like it was one good gust of wind away from toppling over or collapsing in on itself. I would have thought the place was really abandoned too had I been an ordinary passerby under normal circumstances. But these were not normal circumstances.

They were anything but. I knew exactly what I would find when I walked through that door. I could feel it in my gut.

I started forward and headed down the little slope toward the cabin.

CHAPTER TWENTY-NINE

ARCHER

The inside of the cabin was just how I imagined it would look, judging from its state on the outside.

Scarce furniture littered the place—an old couch and a chair that looked like they were older than my grandma Mabel—were all torn apart, broken, and probably home to a raccoon or two.

The wooden floor, just like the wood outside, looked rotten in certain places, and I could see dead roaches and animal droppings covering things to give it a little extra flavor. This house definitely wasn't going to make it on HGTV anytime soon.

Cobwebs and dust thicker than syrup were the dominant features here. They covered everything.

The kitchen, off to my left, looked like it was home to thousands of different diseases, both known and unknown, and had never been cleaned, even when whoever used to live here occupied it.

That very kitchen was the source of something that had to be dead, judging by the smell. As soon as that thought entered my mind, another one followed immediately, making my blood run ice-cold in my veins.

Slowly, I made my way into the kitchen to see exactly what the source of the smell was, praying harder than I ever had that it really was just a dead animal. Stepping into the kitchen, the smell got stronger until I had to use my jacket's sleeve to cover my nose to keep from gagging.

It smelled awful. Something was definitely dead.

Stepping around a small upturned wooden dining table, which was missing one of its legs, I walked toward the old white fridge in the corner.

The smell got stronger the closer I got to the fridge until I had to do awkward mouth breathing to keep from puking right there on the floor.

Staring at the fridge like it was a ticking time bomb, I slowly reached one hand out and pulled the door open. As soon as the door was opened, the overwhelming smell smacked into me, and my stomach emptied onto the floor.

A fucking possum. There was a dead possum in the fridge. How the hell did that even get in there?

After emptying my stomach on the floor, I quickly closed the fridge and exited the kitchen, trying to get as far away from the stench.

Back in the small living area, I saw that there was nothing else to the tiny cabin. There was a hall right off the living room, which led to the rest of the cabin.

Visible from where I stood was four doors—two on the right and two on the left, and a small window at the end of the hall that looked out into the dense forest surrounding the cabin.

Slowly, I made my down the hall and opened the first door on my right. It was a bedroom. Or it used to be. The mattress and all other furnishings were long gone. The only thing left was the old metal frame for the bed.

I was pretty sure Gemma wasn't in here, but just for good measure, I checked the small closet toward the back of the room and found nothing but more dust and dead bugs.

Exiting the room and out into the hall, I could see that the room right across was a bathroom as the slightly opened door showed a toilet that just like the rest of the stuff in this damn cabin, had seen better days.

Passing by it without checking, I came to the second and last door on the right and found a padlock on the door. My heart, already hammering loudly, picked up its pace.

I placed my ear to the door, trying to see if I could hear anything.

There was nothing.

I knocked a few times with my ear still placed on the door.

"Gemma?" I called out as loud as I dared.

Although the cabin was small, and I was pretty sure that jackass wasn't here, I didn't want to take my chances. I hadn't exactly been quiet when I entered the cabin, and if he had been here, I was sure he would have made an appearance by now. There was still one more door to check, and although the chances were slim, for all I knew, he could be behind that one.

But Gemma, I knew she had to be behind this one.

"Gemma?" I called out to her again, a little louder this time.

Still no response. I cursed before looking down at the padlock on the door.

I had to get in there.

Turning away, I quickly ran back outside and searched around.

Finding what I was looking for, I hurried over to pick up the decent-sized rock that had caught my eye and hurried back inside. Back in front of the door, I took a deep breath before slamming the rock down onto the lock three times before it broke and gave way.

Dropping the rock, I made quick work of the lock and flung the door open. Inside was pitch black, and I couldn't see much.

"Gemma?" I called once again. Just like before, there was no answer.

Taking a few steps into the room, I felt along the wall. I ran my hand up and down until it caught on the light switch. A single bulb in the center of the ceiling illuminated the room, and my heart dropped at the sight in front of me.

There was Gemma, her right foot chained to the bottom post of an old bed, beaten almost beyond recognition. Even from the door, I could see the blood and bruises that littered her face and body. Her shirt was missing, leaving her in nothing but her bra and the shorts and flips flops I saw her in before she was taken.

I started to feel sick to my stomach again. What had he done to her?

Taking a few steps across the room until I was on the side of the bed and in front of her, I looked down at her, and it was so much worse.

He had nearly beaten her to death from the looks of it. I could barely recognize her face.

I felt the telltale stinging behind my eyes and the feeling in my throat like I had swallowed a wad of cotton as I looked down at her.

She had gone through who knows what kind of hell at the hands of that bastard, and she did it all alone.

Alone and terrified.

I knew the type of person he was and the type of damage he could do. The worst part? I wasn't there to do a damn thing about it.

I tried to clear my head of these thoughts that threatened to bring me to my knees.

I had a job to do now.

I may not have been able to stop this from happening to her, but I sure as hell was going to get her out of here. I knelt down and slowly reached out and placed a hand on her shoulder, which was ice-cold.

I gently shook her. "Gemma?" I called softly. My voice sounded strained even to my own ears.

No response.

I shook her gently again. She didn't even budge.

A new type of fear washed over me and froze me to the spot as I looked at her closely. Was . . . was she breathing?

Panic and ice-cold fear started to take over as I shook her a little harder this time.

"Gemma. Gemma, please."

She wasn't dead. She couldn't be. She just . . . couldn't be.

When there was still no response, I placed both hands on her shoulders and shook her again.

"Gemma?!"

I don't think I had ever been so happy to hear that small groan of pain that came from her lips just then. I exhaled heavily and reached up to cup her cheek as she slowly turned her head toward me.

"Gemma, can you hear me?"

I watched as she slowly opened her eyes despite them being almost shut, and I almost cried when those blue eyes made contact with mine.

My relief was short-lived, though, as I watched complete fear overtake her features. She instantly tried to move out of my reach and toward the other side of the bed.

"No, please!" she screamed, her voice hoarse like she had been doing nothing but screaming since she was brought here.

I tried to reach out to her. "Gem—"

"Please leave me alone! Don't touch me!"

My heart shattered as she cowered away from me.

"I'll listen. I-I'll do what you want. Please just . . . just don't hurt me anymore."

The last part was just a broken whisper as tears fell from her eyes. Tears that matched my own as I got a glimpse of the extent of the hell she had been put through. I swallowed hard and reached out to her again, cupping her cheek. I tried to ignore her flinch as she turned away.

"Baby," I began softly. "I-it's me. Archer."

Slowly, as if it was taking time for the pieces to be put together in her head, she turned back to look at me, confusion apparent on her face.

"A-Archer?" she questioned quietly.

I nodded. "It's me."

Recognition and then relief crossed her battered features before she started crying even harder before she leaned forward to lock her arms around my neck, burying her head in my shoulder. I felt the sobs that wracked her body.

I wrapped my arms around her, careful not to squeeze her too hard, and gently stroked her hair.

"It's okay, baby. I'm here." But it wasn't okay. Not really.

Whatever he had done to her, the damage was already done. She would have a hard time recovering from this, but I would make sure I was there every step of the way.

She pulled back, and I felt a pain in my chest as I looked her over—bloodied and bruised face and busted lip.

"H-how did you get here? How did you find me?" she asked, looking at me like she expected all this to be a dream and that I would disappear at any second.

I gently ran my thumb over the bruise covering her left cheek before looking her in the eyes.

"I'd go through hell and high water to get to you. Nothing was going to stop me from finding you. Nothing." And I meant it. There was no way I would stop until I found her and had her in my arms again.

I watched in despair as more tears fell from her eyes, and my heart broke even more as she attempted to smile at me but couldn't fully because of the pain in her face.

"Thank you," she whispered.

I pulled her back and hugged her as tightly as I dared. I allowed myself a few more seconds to simply relish in the fact that I had found her and that she was alive before I pulled back.

137

We couldn't waste any more time here. Who knew how long we had until he came back?

"I'm going to get you out of here, okay?"

She nodded weakly.

There was only one problem. I stood up and looked down at her chained foot. How was I going to get her out of that?

I looked back into the hall at the rock I had used earlier but quickly dismissed the idea. There was no way I could do that without shattering her ankle.

I needed something sharp.

I turned back to Gemma. "I'll be right back, okay?"

The instant fear that overtook her features nearly broke me.

"Where are you going?" she asked, her eyes wide as she started frantically looking around the room.

I quickly knelt back in front of her and brought her face close to mine. "I'm not going to leave you. I just need to find something to get that off you," I said, gesturing to her shackled ankle. I leaned in and pressed a kiss to her forehead. "I'll be back. Okay?"

I saw her bottom lip tremble before she nodded.

I got to my feet again and made my way to the door. Before leaving the room, I looked back at Gemma again, sitting in the middle of the bed, looking like a scared child.

"I'll be back. I promise."

She nodded again and responded quietly, "Okay."

I took a deep breath before exiting the room. I needed to find something to get her out of those chains, but I didn't exactly have a large set of options to choose from in this tiny cabin.

I glanced to my right at the last door I still hadn't checked.

Making my way over, I pulled the door open and stopped short. The door led down into a basement. I wasn't exactly a fan of going down into dark, creepy basements in tiny cabins in the middle of the woods.

I glanced back at the room where Gemma was waiting. I was going to do it anyway.

Before I descended, I flipped the switch on, on the wall to my left, and the light bathed the steps in a creepy yellow glow.

Once I made it to the bottom, there was another light switch to my right that I switched on, and my blood ran cold for what probably was the third or fourth time in thirty minutes as I looked at what was in front of me.

There was a single metal table, like the ones that medical examiners would lay dead bodies on, in the middle of the floor, directly over a drain. Attached to each leg of the table were chains with a shackle at each end. On the wall behind the table was an assortment of wicked-looking tools.

Various knives, needles, pliers, a saw. Everything one needed to torture someone was here.

I felt bile rise in my throat.

Looking at how clean everything was, he hadn't had the chance to use any of it yet, but the fact that he planned to on Gemma made me want to puke.

We had to get the hell out of here and fast.

I quickly snatched the saw from the wall before running back up the steps, taking two at a time. I ran back into the room and instantly felt bad as Gemma nearly jumped out of her skin as I came rushing back into the room.

She looked at the saw in my hand with confusion. "Where'd you find that?"

I shook my head as I instantly started sawing at the chain.

"It was just lying around," I said, unwilling to let Gemma know what exactly that monster had planned for her.

It took a few minutes of hard sawing, but I sawed through the metal eventually. The saw was new, apparently. As soon as the chain snapped, I dropped the saw and wiped the sweat covering my forehead.

I turned to Gemma and gave her a small smile.

"Let's get you out of here."

Walking to her end of the bed, I quickly discarded my jacket and draped it over her shoulders to cover her.

I leaned forward to gently scoop her up in my arms, knowing there was probably no way she could walk right now, and looked down into her eyes to find her already looking back up at me.

"Archer?" she said, her voice small as I lifted her from the bed and into my arms.

"Hm?" I asked as I adjusted her in my arms.

"I love you."

I froze at those three words, looking into her eyes and knowing she meant them wholeheartedly.

I pulled her even closer to my chest. "I love you too, baby."

She gave a small smile before leaning her head against my shoulder.

I exited the room with Gemma in my arms, fully prepared to walk her through the woods and back to safety at the hotel, but froze in my tracks as soon as I made it out into the hall.

In the doorway and blocking our one and only exit stood Sheep Mask. He said nothing at first, just stood there silently staring at us through the eye holes in his mask.

We stood there silently staring at each other until he shook his head and raised the knife I had failed to notice.

"It looks like you're trying to take what's mine."

CHAPTER THIRTY

This could not be happening. Not again.

Every time we were almost in the clear, this bastard would magically show up. It was almost like he could tell our next move, before we even made it.

Slowly, wary of any moves he would make, I glanced around. My eyes flitted around the hall and then up, and sure enough, in the left corner, right above the basement door, was a camera pointed into the room where he kept Gemma. Continuing my search, I found another right above the door that Sheep Mask was standing in front of and then another at the kitchen entrance.

Damnit! How did I not notice them before?

I heard a dark chuckle and tore my eyes away from the cameras and back to the man that was literally becoming my walking nightmare.

"Are you just now noticing my toys?" he asked. Sheep Mask shook his head. "I have others that are a lot more fun to play with that I'm simply dying to show you." Sheep Mask's head turned in the direction of the basement door.

I tightened my grip on Gemma, who, during this entire exchange, hadn't uttered a single word.

"What do you say, huh? How about we take a little trip downstairs and introduce Gemma to my new toys since you've already seen them?"

Gemma finally moved as she turned her head slightly to look up at me with wide, fearful, and questioning eyes.

I tried to ignore her eyes as I stared straight ahead at Sheep Mask.

"Like hell, we will. We're not going anywhere with you," I said through clenched teeth. I would be damned if I let him hurt her again.

Sheep Mask chuckled again. Like anything about this situation was funny. "Is that a challenge boy?"

I froze at his words.

The way he just spoke. It reminded me of . . . Suddenly, I was back on the train where all this mess had started. I was sitting with Gemma to my right, and Dox was standing right in front of me, pressing the barrel of his gun to my forehead after I hadn't answered his question. He was pissed, which seemed to be his default mood.

"Have you lost your tongue now, boy? I'm talking to you. Now is the time when you speak."

Those words swarmed around in my head like angry bees as I stared ahead at Sheep Mask.

That voice. It was all coming back to me at once like a punch to the gut. It couldn't be. Could it?

"You putting two and two together now, boy?"

I couldn't form any words. There was no way.

Gemma, who hadn't seemed to have put the pieces together yet, was slowly looking between Sheep Mask and me with a worried expression on her face.

"Archer? What's wrong?"

I swallowed hard as I continued to stare at him.

"It's you, isn't it?" I asked, finally able to speak.

Sheep Mask chuckled and simply shook his head. "This isn't really how I wanted to do my big reveal, but I guess it'll do," he said as he slowly reached up and grabbed the bottom of his mask.

142

In a few seconds, he had pulled the mask off his face revealing a face I still saw in my sleep. It only left me more confused.

Staring at me was definitely the face that belonged to Sheep Mask when we were down in the tunnels. The dark hair and brown eyes, even down to the crooked nose.

So, why was he acting as if he were someone else?

Sheep Mask, or what used to be Sheep Mask, took a few slow steps into the room with a smile plastered on his face.

"Still trying to process things I see. Well, I'll make it simple for you both." He held his hands out wide like he was expecting a hug. "Why don't you two come over here and greet your old pal Dox, hm?"

I took a few steps back, my grip on Gemma tightening.

"You're not Dox. I killed him," I said, shaking my head. "You're the guy who was wearing that Sheep Mask the entire time we were down there."

He simply shook his head and made a *tsk, tsk* sound with his mouth.

"But have you actually seen Dox's face? How can you compare us both when you've only seen one person's face?"

My head was spinning. None of this made any sense.

"You look like your brain's working overtime over there, boy." He laughed. "I'll go ahead and put you out of your misery and lay it all out there for you."

The sick bastard was enjoying this. He was acting like this whole thing was one big story time.

"When we first met on the train, you were a mouthy little bastard," he began while glaring at me. "You see, I hate when people talk back, and the minute you opened your mouth, I knew I was going to have to do something about that. I had an entire plan when I came down into the tunnels. I had been working on it for months, but I changed it all just for you."

143

He gave me a sick smirk. "So, the minute everyone took off down those tracks, I switched masks with the original guy who was wearing this mask." He held up the mask in his hand. "And I went after you on my own. When we ran into each other the first time down in those tunnels after you stupidly came running because you heard a little girl's scream. That was me behind that mask. It was also me when we got into our little . . . scuffle," he said through clenched teeth, clearly irritated that I had gotten the best of him back then."

Gemma finally spoke up. "That can't be true. Dox was the one who took me from that room and tied me to those pipes."

Dox simply shook his head. "No, sweetheart. That was simply one of my guys wearing the mask you first saw me in. They were all playing along. Couldn't have you guys figuring out that we had switched masks now, could I? That would have ruined all the fun."

Dox gave a big sigh. "Unfortunately, you ruined it anyway. The plan was for you to be led back to the waiting platform where you were supposed to be burned alive in that train car while I watched through video from another room. Imagine my surprise when you actually killed one of my men." You could practically hear the venom dripping from his voice.

"By the time I got back to the waiting platform, you and the other boy were already long gone, and I'm not stupid. I knew I was outnumbered then. So, I just bid my time. After listening to your stories on the news, I knew the little punk with the nose ring would be my best chance to get to you. It only took a little threatening and blackmail to get him to do what I needed, and now here we are," Dox finished with his arms spread wide.

"So, the guy I killed . . ." I began.

"That was the original guy in this mask here," Dox said, gesturing to the mask again. "Not me."

I felt like I had just been hit over the head with a brick.

Looking back, I guess it did all make sense. Sheep Mask didn't have the same obsession with us as Dox did. Come to think of it, the entire time we were interacting with Sheep Mask, if what he said was true, we were actually interacting with Dox.

I think we just assumed because we had killed his friend, ruined their entire plan, and left him down there to rot, that it was really him who had come back to get his revenge.

Dox stopped the pacing he had been doing while he was recounting his story and simply stood there, twirling the knife in his hand.

"Well, now that story time is over, where were we?" As Dox began to take slow steps forward, I took matching steps back.

I looked down at Gemma, who was watching Dox slowly advance with a terrified look on her face. She couldn't go through anything else.

I wouldn't let her.

"When I tell you to, run," I whispered, not taking my eyes off Dox.

Gemma tore her gaze away from Dox and looked at me with wide eyes. "What? No, I—"

"Gemma, please. I'm not going to let him hurt you again. When I tell you to, you run. Understand?"

She opened her mouth like she wanted to argue but then closed it and nodded once. Slowly, I set her on her feet, and instead of continuing to step back, I took a step forward.

Dox cocked his head to the side. "Finally grown a pair?" he taunted.

I took a deep breath. "Guess there's only one way to find out, isn't there?"

Before he could respond, I charged forward.

In the blink of an eye, I collided with him, and we tumbled to the floor. Conscious of the knife he still held, I attempted to wrestle it out of his hand. While he was occupied, I looked over my shoulder at Gemma, who looked like a deer caught in headlights.

145

"Run!"

She only hesitated for a second before she darted past us. Once she reached the door, however, she stopped completely, turning back to look at me with a torn look on her face. I knew what she was thinking.

"Gemma, go! I'll be okay. Just get out of here and get to the police. They're at the hotel."

I watched as she bit her bottom lip, that torn look still on her face.

"Archer—"

"Go!"

She jumped a little at my tone before she turned and ran out the door and down the steps. I felt a wave of relief flow through me as I watched her disappear.

She was safe.

My relief was short-lived, however, as I felt Dox's fist connect with my face, effectively knocking me backward and on my ass.

Before I even had time to get my bearings, he was kneeling over me with his knife pressed to my throat.

"You'll pay for that." He quickly glanced over his shoulder at the door Gemma had just run through, then back down at me. "I'll just find her again, but in the meantime, I think it's time you and I got to know each other a little better."

He slapped me roughly on the cheek.

"Let's go introduce you to those new toys I bought."

CHAPTER THIRTY-ONE

ARCHER

Dox grabbed me roughly by the root of my hair before harshly pulling me to my feet, his grip tight.

He didn't bother uttering another word as he pressed the edge of the blade he was holding into my lower back and then proceeded to push me forward, and we silently began to descend the stairs one at a time.

The sound of my feet hitting each step echoed in time to the sound of my blood rushing and my heartbeat thrumming in my ears.

This was probably it.

I figured I had used up all the luck I was due at this point. There was no getting out this time.

I was only thankful I had found Gemma and got her out of this hellhole before it happened. No matter how things went down, she was safe, and that was all that mattered to me now.

After I stepped off the stairs, my focus was forced back on my current situation as I looked at what lay before me. I was once again in the basement surrounded by all the tools Dox had set up to use for his sick pleasure.

On me.

"Looks like a lot of fun, doesn't it?" Dox breathed.

I could actually hear the excitement in his voice. He really got off on stuff like this.

Sick bastard.

He pressed the blade into my lower back harder as he ushered me toward the table in the center of the room. Once I was in front of it, I felt the blade leave my back and glanced over my shoulder, only to find it pointed right in my face.

"Get on the table."

It wasn't a request. It was a demand.

Gritting my teeth, I turned and looked down at the table before me. This was where I was going to die. Of all the ways to die, this was probably the worst.

There wasn't much I could do about it though.

So, instead, I took a deep breath before slowly climbing onto the table and lay down on my back. I felt like a fucking lab experiment, which I guess, I kind of was.

I refused to make eye contact with him as he began to walk around each corner of the table, securing my hands and feet to each corner. Before long, I was completely vulnerable to whatever this bastard planned to do to me. The thought did nothing but add to the cold sweat that had broken out across my skin.

My heart was now beating rapidly beneath my rib cage.

I tried to ignore the sounds Dox was making as he fumbled with something behind me. Metal clanging against metal echoed around the small room, making me clench my fists. I tried to control my breathing and keep myself calm, but it was no use.

I was terrified.

Suddenly, Dox's face was hovering right above mine, making me jump back, or my body attempted to anyway. There was nowhere to escape to, tied to this damned table.

"Let's begin then, shall we?" Dox said, his voice full of dark intent.

I followed him with my eyes as he rolled a smaller table near my head and then proceeded to lay out a series of silver-colored tools on the smaller table. My eyes landed on the handsaw that sat among all the tools. Dox must have noticed where my eyes were looking as he smiled wickedly down at me.

"You like that one, do you?"

My eyes followed as he picked up the saw, held it up, and slowly began to turn it over in his hand, examining it.

"It's a beauty, isn't it?" Dox paused his inspection of the saw and looked directly into my eyes. "It cuts right through skin and bone like a knife through softened butter."

My heart was beating so fast it was now painful as he placed the flat part of the saw right above my shoulder and then slowly trailed it down my arm. The cold sting of the metal on my skin caused goosebumps to rise over my flesh before he paused with the saw right over my right wrist.

"Would you like a demonstration?"

I clenched my teeth and my fists as I stared back at him. I was not going to give the bastard the satisfaction of replying. What the hell did he want me to say? *"Yes, I'd love for you to show me exactly how you plan to cut my fucking hand off?"*

He would have a better chance of waiting for hell to freeze over.

"Not going to answer, huh?" He shrugged. "That's fine. I'll get you talking soon enough."

He put the saw back on the table and instead picked up a pair of scissors. Without another word, he placed the scissors at the hem of my T-shirt then proceeded to cut upward. It fell uselessly to the side, exposing my torso completely as he cut all the way to the neckline.

Then he turned away, returned the scissors to the table, and replaced them with a sharp knife with a curved blade at the end.

Dox only glanced at me once, that devilish smirk still on his face, before he ran the blade across my pectoral muscles end to end.

I couldn't keep the scream that tore from me as the blade cut through my flesh. The feeling of warm liquid across my skin instantly followed the pain after the cuts he made.

Dox pulled the knife away, smiling in satisfaction as he looked down at his work.

However, that was only the beginning.

The pain and my screams only increased as he continued to dig the knife into different places of my exposed chest and arms.

By the time he finally decided to pull the blade away, my skin was covered in red. The cuts were not deep enough to kill, at least not right then anyway, but they were deep enough to draw significant amount of blood. My blood dripped down in a steady flow from the various cuts. The sound of it hitting the floor made me nauseous.

My breathing was labored, hair plastered to my forehead with sweat, but Dox just gave a dark and humorless laugh as he looked at my state.

"Don't tell me you're ready to tap out already. We're just getting started, boy."

I didn't bother replying. Any energy I had, was now used to try and fight to stay alive for as long as I could. I heard the clang as Dox placed the knife that was now covered in blood, my blood, back on the table.

What he picked up next made me wish that maybe I was already dead. I felt the cold sting of the saw on my right wrist again and then on my pinky finger before he applied pressure and cut straight through flesh and bone, severing my finger.

The sound that escaped my throat as he was cutting my finger was nonhuman.

Dox picked up my severed finger and held it up to the light before waving it right in front of my face.

My stomach rolled, and seconds later, I was throwing up. Since I couldn't bend over, I turned my head to the side to try and keep most of the vomit from landing on my chest or choking me.

Dox laughed again, this time louder. He placed my finger down on the tools' table before moving toward the other end, the saw still in his hand.

"Well, that was a finger. How about a toe this time?"

Panic surged through me as he began untying my right shoe before he removed it and then my sock. I strained against the chains, trying to move away as he grabbed my ankle and pressed the cold saw against one of my toes, but it was no use.

I couldn't go anywhere. I couldn't stop him.

I couldn't do anything but lay there and let this sick fuck do whatever the hell he wanted. I screwed my eyes shut and gritted my teeth so hard I thought they might shatter as I felt him begin to press the saw down again.

However, the pain only lasted a second. The pressure of the saw against my toe disappeared. Instead of another digit getting cut off, a loud thump followed by a grunt and then another thud happened.

I opened my eyes, trying to figure out what the hell he was doing now, but instead of Dox, I was met with the wild and wide blue gaze of Gemma, holding a large rock over her head with both hands as she stood over Dox who now lay in an unconscious heap on the floor.

"Gemma?" My voice was nothing more than a hoarse whisper.

She tore her gaze away from Dox to look at me and instantly dropped the rock before rushing to my side.

"Archer," she gave a horrified whisper as she looked me over, and an instant feeling of déjà vu hit me.

I probably looked the same as she did when I had found her not that long ago. Her eyes ran all over my chest and arms and then down to my right hand before they widened in horror.

"Oh my God," she whispered.

151

She looked back up at me, tears now falling down her cheeks. She glanced around the room and hurried over to the wall behind me that held all the tools.

"What are you doing?" I muttered as I tried to follow her movements, but I could only strain my head so far.

"I have to find something to get you out of here."

I heard her fumbling through the different tools before she stopped, and her face appeared in my field of vision again, only she had nothing in her hands.

I gave her a questioning glance before she looked down at Dox. Without another word, she bent over him and began searching his pockets.

"What are you doing?" My voice now sounded slurred and weak.

I was losing a lot of blood.

Gemma said nothing and continued to rummage through his pockets before she gave a triumphant shout and stood up, holding a small shiny piece of metal.

A key.

He really kept the damn key in his pocket. Again. I guess old habits died hard.

Gemma made quick work of unlocking both my feet and my left arm. However, when she got to my right arm, she froze. Her hands trembled a little as she held them above my right hand, now missing my pinky finger.

Weakly, but with all the strength I had left, I reached over with my left hand and gently grabbed the key from her hand.

She looked at me, crying again, and silently shook her head. "I'm so sorry. If you hadn't come to find me, this—"

"Don't you dare," I cut her off as I inserted the key and made quick work of the chains around my right wrist before it sprang open, and I was free.

Once the chains fell away from my wrist, I looked back up at Gemma and made sure she was looking at me before I continued, "I'd let that fucker cut off all my fingers one hundred times over if it meant saving you."

It only served to make her cry harder.

If blood wasn't covering me and cuts didn't decorate almost every inch of my torso, I would have pulled her to me in a crushing hug.

"Let's get out of here," I muttered instead.

Gemma nodded and moved to help me as I slowly swung my feet over the edge of the table and *tried* to stand. As soon as my feet hit the ground, however, and I went to stand up, my vision swam, and I swayed before collapsing back onto the table.

I really had lost too much blood.

She noticed this too as she looked down at my chest and hand. Without hesitation, she started pulling the remnants of my shirt off my body.

"Gemma, I know I'm hard to resist, but do you really think now's the right time for this?" I joked lamely.

She only gave me an exasperated look and shook her head.

"How can you even still joke around right now?" she asked as she took my shirt off and wrapped it around my right hand as gently as possible.

It didn't stop it from hurting like hell, though. I gritted my teeth, a painful groan still managing to escape. Gemma gave me an apologetic look as she finished wrapping my hand and then helped me to stand again, slower this time. My vision was still swimming with dark spots, but I managed to stay on my feet this time.

Supporting my weight, she led me to the steps, making a wide berth around Dox, who still lay unconscious on the floor, or maybe he was dead, judging from the small pool of blood slowly spreading from his head.

Almost sensing my thoughts, Gemma paused at the bottom of the steps and looked over her shoulder at him.

"Gemma?" I questioned.

153

She swallowed before looking at me. "I don't want to make the same mistake twice. We need to kill him."

"Gemma, you d—"

"I do. If I had just listened to you before, and we had killed him back then, none of this would have happened."

She didn't even give me a chance to reply. She positioned me so that I was braced against the railing of the stairs before walking over to the large rock she had used to knock him out the first time. I watched as she picked it up and then stood over his body. Slowly, she raised the rock over her head. Her hands were trembling.

"Gemma." I tried to reason with her again.

She wasn't a killer, no matter the circumstances. If she did this, she wouldn't be able to come back from it, no matter what she said.

"I can do this," she whispered, but she wasn't talking to me.

She was trying to convince herself. She shut her eyes tight and, after five seconds, opened them again, a determined glint now in her eyes.

She was going to do it. She was really going to kill him. She pulled her arms back as far as she could, fully prepared to bring the rock down and end his life.

However, right as she got ready to do just that, a shout of, "Police! Is there anybody in here?!"

Gemma froze. Her wide gaze met mine before she looked back down at Dox.

"Anybody down there?"

The sound of the police officer's voice was closer now. He sounded as if he was right at the open door that led down into the basement.

"Hello?!" he called down.

Gemma exhaled deeply before dropping the rock. It landed with a thud next to his head. How lucky for him.

Gemma silently made her way back over to me and once again let me use her as support.

"We're down here!"

CHAPTER THIRTY-TWO

GEMMA

"We're down here!"

There was only a brief moment of silence before heavy booted footfalls were quickly descending the steps, and not long after, an officer with short dark hair cut close to his head and a pair of dark eyes to match came into view.

I was sure we were a sight to see because his eyes widened when he made it to the bottom step and fully took in the sight of us.

"Jesus Christ," he whispered to himself, confirming my thoughts, as he looked us over before quickly pulling a radio from his side. "This is Sanchez. I've found them," he spoke into the radio.

There was another brief moment of silence. This one a little more awkward as no one uttered a single word. We simply stood there staring at one another before the two-tone *beep* of the walkie-talkie, followed by another voice, broke it once again.

"Copy that, Sanchez. What is your location?"

Officer Sanchez quickly described our location to the person over the walkie-talkie before putting it back in its place on his hip.

"I'd ask if you two were okay, but I can already see the answer. So, let's just get you two out of here, okay?"

I simply nodded. The sooner we got out of here, the better. Archer was losing a lot of blood, and he was swaying on his feet so much I was worried if he could even make it up the steps.

There was one thing that needed to be handled first, though.

"I can get Archer up the stairs myself, but you have to stay with him." I gestured over my shoulder toward the man who was responsible for nearly destroying my life.

Twice.

Officer Sanchez followed my action with his eyes to Dox, lying in an unconscious heap on the floor. I watched the unasked question form in his eyes as he looked back from Dox to us again.

"He's responsible for this," I answered his unasked question. "He did this to us." I gestured toward both myself and Archer, a feeling of disgust and anger taking over as I looked at the poor excuse for a human being who would do something so horrible to another person.

Officer Sanchez only nodded once, understanding clear in his eyes, before he walked over to Dox's body. He reached for his belt, ready to grab the pair of handcuffs, when he suddenly froze, his face going a little pale.

I tried to figure out exactly what was wrong as he stared not down at Dox but at something else.

"Is that—"

I followed his hand, pointing to something to his left and suddenly realized what had him looking like he might lose his lunch at any second.

"That's my finger." Archer's voice cut through the silence.

Officer Sanchez's gaze landed on Archer and then slowly made its way down to his right arm and then to his hand, now wrapped in the tattered remains of his shirt that was quickly soaking through with his blood.

Sanchez swallowed hard once, then quickly handcuffed Dox before pulling out his radio again.

"This is Sanchez. We're going to need a cooler here. Kid lost his finger."

Archer scoffed, still swaying on his feet. He looked like he might pass out any second now. "I didn't lose my fucking finger. That bastard cut it off."

Officer Sanchez actually looked lost for words as he repeatedly opened his mouth and then closed it.

I couldn't really blame him. Archer did have the tendency to make a person speechless. I gently squeezed his left hand and gestured toward the stairs.

"Let's go."

Slowly we began to make our way up the steps, and it was apparent just how much blood Archer had lost because he barely had any strength to climb the first few steps.

Before we were able to make it to the top, I glanced over my shoulder one last time.

"Make sure you watch him," I called down, looking directly at Officer Sanchez.

If we made the same mistake twice, it would just be another repeat of what happened today, and I couldn't go through this again.

"Don't take your eyes off of him."

Officer Sanchez nodded.

"Don't worry. He's not going anywhere."

I looked at Dox's body before turning back around. I hoped not.

*   *   *

Once we had made it outside, it wasn't like I could drag Archer all the way back through the woods the way we had come.

He wouldn't make it.

So, instead, I found a tree a little ways from the cabin, where we could sit at its base while we waited for the police to

158

come. As gently as I could, I helped Archer settle himself against the tree before I sat next to him.

His eyes were starting to flutter, rolling toward the back, and were going in and out of focus.

"I'm exhausted," he mumbled tiredly, his head lolling to the side to lean against my shoulder.

"I know. Just stay up with me until the police get here, okay?"

I felt him nod against my shoulder.

I was worried that if he fell asleep, he might not wake up. I needed to keep him conscious until help arrived.

"How'd you find me?" I asked, hoping that talking would keep him up.

I felt his body shake against mine as he laughed a little.

"A floating squirrel."

I frowned and looked at him, convinced the blood loss had really taken its toll on him.

"A what?" I asked, trying to make sure I had heard him right.

Archer turned to look at me, a small smile on his face, before he turned back to look out at the woods in front of him.

"There was a floating squirrel. Well, I thought it was a floating squirrel at first, but it was just sitting on top of that white van covered in camouflage netting."

I nodded as I finally made sense of what he was talking about.

"Honestly, it was just luck," he continued. "If I hadn't seen that squirrel, I probably never would've noticed the van. I was just wandering around out here hoping I'd find you."

"And you did."

Archer's gaze met mine, that soft smile still on his face. "I did."

159

I smiled back at him before leaning over and pressing a kiss on his cheek. "You've saved my ass more times than I care to count."

His body shook as he laughed again. "Should I start making a list?"

I turned to look at the small abandoned cabin that had been home to my living nightmare.

"No. Let's hope this was the last time."

I felt his hand slowly close around mine, drawing my attention from the cabin and back to him.

"It was."

I simply nodded before another question popped into my head. "How'd you make it out of there? I thought you died when the building exploded," I said, remembering the utter despair I felt as I watched the hotel become engulfed in smoke and flames.

I felt Archer shake his head. "I wasn't inside when the building exploded. I was already outside, headed in the direction the van had gone."

I frowned at that.

"What about your phone?"

"What about it?"

"You're phone didn't explode?"

"Why would my phone explode?"

I could hear the confusion in his voice. I quickly explained what Dylan had told me earlier, and after listening, it was like a lightbulb turned on.

"I think I accidentally dropped it on my way up the stairs when I was leaving the building."

I looked at Archer in astonishment. He had been so close to death, and he hadn't even known it. It was only his carelessness about his phone that saved him. I had watched him drop it several times since we had been together, and it was a wonder that thing even still worked.

"Jesus, Archer. You were so close to dying."

160

Archer lazily raised his eyebrow at me. "That's nothing new."

I opened my mouth to respond, but the sounds of several footsteps rushing toward us cut me off. In a second, a dozen or so police officers came into view, followed by a few medics carrying stretchers and first aid bags.

I quickly flagged them down. The paramedics and a few officers made their way over to us while the others made their way inside the cabin. I watched as, once again, the sight of us made their eyes widen as they took in the full extent of our injuries.

I had been trying to ignore my own pains, because getting Archer out of there was my only concern. However, now that I knew he would get the help he needed, it felt like all the pain my body had endured came rushing back all at once like a punch to the gut.

I was barely listening to what the medics or the police were saying or doing to me. All I was aware of was that one minute I was sitting against the base of the tree, and the next, I was carried on a stretcher by two medics.

As they got ready to carry us back through the woods and to the ambulance that they had parked beyond the treeline since they couldn't drive through the thick foliage, I felt a gentle brush against my right hand. I turned my head, seeing Archer in the stretcher next to mine, his hand outstretched towards mine.

He didn't say anything. He simply squeezed my hand gently and nodded as if to say, *"Everything's okay now."*

And this time, I truly hoped it would be.

EPILOGUE

The temperature inside the courtroom was freezing.

The AC felt like it was on thirty. It was so cold in here I was sitting here shivering. Or maybe it wasn't the cold that had me shaking in my seat on the wooden bench. It could very well be the fact that the man who had caused me so much pain, so much grief, and so much heartache in such a short amount of time was finally being sentenced today.

A day I never thought I would see.

Not that long ago I wasn't even sure if I was going to live, and now, well now, I was going to see the man who was the cause of it all locked away.

And after everything, he most definitely had it coming.

*　　*　　*

Two weeks ago

Waking up in a hospital was not my favorite pastime. And yet this was already the second time it had happened, and the reason behind it all was the same.

Glancing down, I wasn't surprised to see the various tubes connected to my arms that led to IVs, nor the bandages I could both see and feel covering various parts of my body. Reaching up slowly, I brought the tips of my fingers to my cheek and instantly winced.

There was no doubt I looked as bad as I felt.

"Honey, you're awake."

I turned my head to the side where my mom, who had obviously been sleeping, was now getting up from her spot in what had to be the world's most uncomfortable-looking chair.

How did she get any sleep in that?

My mother rushed over to me and lifted her hands like she wanted to touch me but instantly thought better of it as she looked me over and silently dropped her hands to her side.

I must have really looked bad. I reached out and grabbed one of her hands.

"It's okay. I'm not going to fall apart if you touch me." I attempted a weak smile, but even that tiny movement brought on almost unbearable amounts of pain.

Seeing me winced, my mom's eyes instantly filled with tears. "I'm so sorry, baby," she whispered as silent tears began to fall.

My heart clenched at the sight. "Mom, none of this is your fault."

She shook her head, bringing her hand to her mouth to muffle her sob.

"It is. I let you go on that trip against my better judgment. I knew something bad was going to happen. I felt it the moment you got on the plane."

I shook my head. "There's no way you could've known what was going to happen."

"Maybe not exactly, but you're my baby girl. I know when there's something wrong when it concerns you."

"Mom." My own voice was wavering, and I could feel the tell-tale sting behind my eyes.

"And I ignored it," she continued, even more tears leaving a trail down her cheeks now. "I ignored it, and look what happened to you. I let my daughter be put in a situation where she had to fight for her life and have had to watch you be brought to a hospital beaten and broken twice."

She couldn't control the sob that escaped this time as she covered her face with her hands. "And this time, it was so much worse." She pulled her hands away to look me straight in the eyes. "Gemma, we didn't know if you were going to wake up. You were unconscious for three days."

163

Three days?! That couldn't be right.

The last thing I remembered was being put on the stretcher once the police had reached me and Archer—

Archer!

"Mom, where's Archer? Is he okay?" *The look on her face made my heart drop.* "Mom?"

She shook her head silently, wiping the tears from her cheeks. "Sweetie, I'm sorry. He . . . he hasn't woken up."

My increased heartbeat reflected on the heart rate monitor in the room. I shook my head.

"Why? What's wrong?"

"I'm not exactly sure. Only family has been allowed in the room with him, but your father spoke to his parents, and they said the doctors told them they did all they could."

No. That couldn't be true. Archer had to be alright. He had to be.

"Honey, he lost a lot of blood. They said it's a miracle that he's even still breathing."

"I have to see him." *I began pulling the tubes from my arms and swung my legs over the side of the bed, ignoring the pain that raced up my rib cage.* "I have to—"

My mom placed a hand on my shoulder. "Gemma, you can't. You're in no condition to be walking around, and even if you were, remember I said they're only letting family members in to see him."

"I am his family."

Those doctors had another thing coming if they thought they could keep me from seeing him. I pulled the last tube from my arm and shakily got to my feet.

As it turns out, I didn't have to worry about the doctors trying to stop me from seeing Archer because my legs did the job for them. The moment I was on my feet my legs instantly gave out and I collapsed in a heap on the floor.

"Gemma!" *My mom was by my side in an instant.* "Are you okay?" *she asked, trying to help me back in the bed, but I wasn't having it.*

I wasn't getting back in any bed until I saw Archer.

"Mom, I have—"

164

Just then the door to my hospital room opened, and I looked up to see my dad standing in the doorway. A shocked look quickly masked the grim one that had been on his face once he saw that I was awake.

"What is it?" my mom asked, clearly having seen the look on his face as well but I knew before my dad even opened his mouth that it was about Archer.

My dad looked at me, a sad look now in his eyes.

"It's Archer. I just spoke to Janet and Michael. He's slipped into a coma."

*　　　*　　　*

Present

Maybe I lied before. Maybe it wasn't the cold or the fact that the man I despised was finally being brought to justice that was making me shiver, but the fact that Archer was still in a coma and not sitting here next to me—where he should have been—to watch it all happen.

Instead, my parents accompanied me. They really hadn't left my side since I woke up in the hospital. And, if for whatever reason, my parents couldn't be right by my side, which wasn't often, Megan was there, always being my rock.

Once I was allowed to leave the hospital, I outright refused to actually do so. I didn't want to leave Archer.

Not if, but when Archer woke up, I wanted to be there.

It was going on day number three, and not even my parents could convince me to leave the spot right outside his room when Megan came marching down the hallway and came to a stop right in front of me with her hands on her hips.

"You look like shit, and you stink. We're going home. Do you want to give him a heart attack when he wakes up?"

And just like that, Megan took me from the hospital.

165

It was during those brief moments when I was with Megan—because I did go back to the hospital after showering and being forced to eat and sleep for a few hours—she explained to me what had happened with her and the others.

Once she woke up, she found that she and the others had all been left in another of the storage rooms that held a bunch of bedding in the basement.

Immediately after the others woke up and realized that both Archer and I were missing, Megan was the first to suggest they go looking for us, and that was what they would have done. But Avery kindly reminded everyone of two things. One, they had no clue where to even begin looking, and two, they could barely even save themselves.

It led to a big argument between Megan and Avery, where Megan claimed she was two seconds away from, *"Punching her in her stupid boob implants."*

Her words, not mine.

Eventually, Cade stepped in and convinced Megan and the others that while they all did want to go looking for us, Avery did have a point. The chances of finding us would be better if they actually got out and found some help instead of mindlessly wandering around down there, especially given the fact that they didn't know exactly who they were up against.

It was this decision that saved all their lives.

So, in a way, I guess I had Avery to thank for saving my best friend's and everyone else's life. A fact that I was sure Avery was never going to let me forget. After getting everyone to agree, they all searched for a way out.

It was only by sheer luck that Dawn tripped over the edge of a rolled-up shag carpet that, upon further inspection, was part of a set of many. They also found a few housekeeping carts, placed strategically so that no one would notice the door that led to the stairs behind it.

The only way anyone would have noticed it was if they knew where to look, to begin with, or in Dawn's case, by being clumsy.

After discovering the stairs, they made quick work clearing the rugs and carts before they all made their way up and outside.

According to Megan, they had only taken a few steps when the basement and bottom floor exploded.

Luckily for them, the group only suffered minor cuts and bruises from the impact of the blast, but others weren't so lucky. Most of those in the lobby and the first floor during the explosion lost their lives. Those on the floors above were able to be safely rescued by the police and fire department.

It was hard to believe that all that death and destruction was caused by a single person. The same person who was now sitting a mere few feet ahead of me, ready to be sentenced.

It had taken weeks, but all the evidence had been presented, and statements of witnesses and victims, mainly my own since Archer couldn't be here, had been given. Going up in front of the entire courtroom and reliving every grueling detail of what Dox had done to me was probably one of the hardest things I have ever had to do.

And the sick part?

The whole time I was recounting what had happened, he sat there smiling at me. As if he was not only reliving but cherishing it. I had never hated and completely loathed another human being the way I did him.

All that was really left now was to see Dox punished for everything he had done, and if he never saw the light of day again, I would be content.

Closing arguments made, it was now the jury and judge's turn to determine his fate.

An older man who looked to be in his mid-to-late fifties, with thinning hair, stood to his feet to address the judge.

The judge, an older woman with a sharp haircut, looked down at the man from her bench. "On the count of kidnapping, how does the jury find the defendant?"

The man wasted no time.

"On the count of kidnapping, we, the jury, find the defendant guilty."

It went on like this for a while, the judge listing all his crimes, each one worse than the last, and the jury finding him guilty for each and every one of them.

It wasn't until they got to his very last crime that my stomach turned into knots. Above all else, this is what I wanted him to pay for the most.

From my right, I felt my mother squeeze my hand.

"On the count of first-degree murder, how does the jury find the defendant?"

"On seven counts of first-degree murder, we, the jury, find the defendant guilty on all counts."

The sick bastard had killed more people than I realized, but as those words left the juror's mouth, it felt like a giant weight was lifted from my shoulders.

Somewhere behind me, I heard a cry of relief and turned my head to see an elderly woman crying into a younger man's shoulder.

She was one of the victims family member, and just like me, she was here to see the man who had obviously taken someone dear to her brought to justice.

At the sound of the judge's voice, I turned around as she addressed the courtroom.

"Found guilty on all accounts, and as the defendant has shown no hint of remorse for his heinous crimes and the lives he's both stolen and destroyed, I hereby sentence the defendant, John Murphy O'Brian to life with no parole."

The sound of the gavel hitting the wooden block echoed around the courtroom.

Everything was a blur after that.

The only thing I really paid attention to was the fact that as Dox (I was never going to be able to think of him as John O'Brian) was being led away by two police officers and right before he disappeared behind the door towards the back of the courtroom, he looked over his shoulder, his eyes making direct contact with mine, and winked.

*　　*　　*

The constant beeping of the heart monitor was the only sound that punctured the otherwise overwhelming silence in the hospital room. It was also the only sound that let me know that Archer was still alive.

As I glanced down at his still face, I could almost pretend that he was only sleeping, and any minute now, he would wake up and bless me with that ever-present smirk and some corny joke.

Almost.

I could almost pretend that, but the reality was that I knew he wasn't just sleeping. His face was too still.

After the sentencing, I immediately made my way back to the hospital to check on Archer's progress, or lack thereof.

I sighed heavily, before I glanced around the hospital room that had become as familiar to me as my own bedroom by now.

Archer's parents, who diligently visited the hospital every day after work to sit by their son's bedside, had stepped out and kindly given me some time alone with Archer even after I had assured them several times they didn't have to.

I looked down at Archer's hand that I gently clasped in my own, trying to ignore how still it felt before speaking.

"It's finally over," I began quietly. "He's going to be locked away for life with no chance of getting out. He's going to pay for everything he had done until the day he dies in there. We can finally live our lives without looking over our shoulders now. So—"

169

The unexpected sting behind my eyes and the lump in my throat kept me from continuing. I let out a small sob and leaned my head against our clasped hands.

"So, please, just wake up now," I pleaded in a broken whisper.

I had pleaded for him to wake up every time I visited, and just like before, my pleas were met with silence.

After sitting there a little longer, I let his parents know they could come back in the room and sit with him for as long as they could before work called them both again.

In the meantime, I decided I would go and get a cup of coffee from the cafeteria because while I was exhausted, there was only so much sleep one could get in those uncomfortable chairs they provided in the hospital room, so I would rather just stay awake as long as my body allowed.

Three hours had passed, and I had just bid Archer's parents goodbye before I took my spot by his bedside again.

Despite the coffee, I found the exhaustion winning out, and before I knew it, my body was slumped over with my head laying on the edge of Archer's bed, his hand once again clasped in my own before my eyes shut and exhaustion took over completely.

When I woke again, it was completely dark outside, letting me know just how much time had passed. I had been asleep long enough that my throat was dry, and my tongue felt like I had just spent a week in the Sahara.

I slowly stood, stretching my limbs and letting out a small groan as my body protested from the awkward position I had slept in before making my way out of the room and walking the short distance down the hall to the small water cooler.

After inhaling the water for the third time from those ridiculously small cups they provided, I filled it for a fourth and final time before heading back to the room, tiny cup in hand.

I had just pushed the door open and taken a few steps into the room when the cup fell from my now limp hand and hit the ground, the small amount of water it held spreading across the floor.

I could hear my heart beating, thumping rapidly against my rib cage, and blood rushing through my veins in my ears as if it was hooked up to a speaker.

Despite the three cups of water I had just downed, my mouth was suddenly dry again.

Green eyes stared back at my own, and the faintest hint of a smirk barely gracing those lips I had come to know like the back of my hand, but it was there.

He was there.

And then he spoke, his voice hoarse from not being used for so long, his voice that I had been dying to hear for so long and was afraid I would never hear again filled the room.

"Guess we're back to you not blinking at me again, huh?"

Do you like thriller stories?
Here are samples of other stories
you might enjoy!

THE Subway

JAE JAE

CHAPTER ONE

I hated riding subways—not just any subway but the subways in New York City, to be exact. I hated those things with an unyielding passion. No ifs, ands, or buts about it.

Who, in their right mind, wanted to ride an underground train that smelled like a kindergartener's tub of stale play dough and old people? Maybe it was just me, maybe I was overexaggerating, or maybe I was losing my sense of smell, but that was definitely the smell that always aggressively assaulted my nose whenever I stepped foot in a subway car.

Then there were the people. I hated how crowded the subways were. I would receive an elbow to the ribs or a hard shove from someone's shoulder almost every time I was forced to ride that thing. At the end of my commute, I always walked out looking like I had just gone ten rounds with a mildly ferocious ten-year-old.

The seating was also a problem. There was never anywhere to sit. If all the seats were taken by the time I got on—and they usually were—then I would be forced to stand among the crowd of swaying bodies, where perverts would "accidentally" rub up against me. It was like a game of musical chairs where the losers would get felt up by a bunch of strange old men as punishment if they could not find a seat in time.

As if all that was not bad enough, the ride itself took at least twenty minutes and I had to ride the damn thing twice.

Why did I have to ride it twice?

Well, that's because I lived right outside my school's district, so technically the school bus could not pick me up from my house. However, I lived close enough that I could walk to the subway station in the city, get a ride, and walk the rest of the way to school every day.

At eighteen, I should be driving back and forth in my own car, but no. My parents, who were definitely using their parent logic on this one, thought it was better that I rode the subway every day, despite the fact that I kept reminding them that I was bound to be kidnapped, robbed, stabbed, or a mix of all three by doing so. We did live in New York, after all. Worse things had happened.

I had made it my job to constantly remind them that when they saw my hideous high school ID picture with the caption "Missing Girl" on the news, it was going to be all their fault.

With all the money I spent riding the subway, I could have bought my own car by now, but did I? No. Apparently, I was not ready for that big of a responsibility yet.

This is where you insert the eye roll and dramatic sigh.

Basically, my parents trusted me to venture into a crowd of people that could easily be hiding serial killers and knife-wielding maniacs—I really needed to quit watching so much *Law and Order*—but they could not trust me with my own car.

Again . . . parent logic.

However, what happened on that one day I rode the subway, that one day that was supposed to be just like any other, I did not think anyone saw it coming.

Not me, not my parents, not the passengers.

No one.

That was the day when I was really in my very own episode of *Law and Order*. I ended up being the victim.

Lucky me.

*　　　*　　　*

Whoever decided to make the iPhone alarm sound like the siren for the end of the world was an idiot. If I did not die from the small heart attacks the stupid thing gave me, then I would end up smashing Satan's creation against my nightstand trying to cut it off.

I was currently on phone number three.

Lucky for my current phone, I was not in a completely hostile mood when it abruptly woke me this time.

Groaning, I blindly slammed my hand down, knocking various items off my nightstand until I found the snooze button, and rolled out of my warm bed.

I landed on the hardwood floor with a loud thud.

My mom's voice rang from downstairs not even two seconds after. "Gemma, what was that? You better not have broken anything!"

Yeah, Mom, don't ask if I was the thing that fell and possibly broke.

I did not even bother getting up or untangling myself from my blanket to answer her. I just rolled over to the door like some sort of deformed giant baked potato and yelled, "It was just a shirt!"

"What kind of shirt makes that sound when it falls?" she yelled back. I could almost picture the deadpan look on her face.

`Did I leave out the part where I was in the shirt when it fell?`

"Well, I'm fine anyway! Thanks for asking!"

"Just hurry up! You're going to be late!" There was a slight pause before she added, "Again!"

Groaning again, I sat up and threw off my blanket, making goose bumps instantly rise on my skin as I was slowly making my way across the hall to the bathroom. I even made extra effort to drag my feet.

Who cared if I was late? Would I really miss out on something important?

Lord forbid I would miss out on my science teacher teaching us the nucleus is the powerhouse of the cell. Or is it the mitochondria?

See? I could not even bother to remember or care that we had learned that years ago. And don't even get me started on the math. I would definitely need to know how to use the quadratic formula later in life.

After showering and doing my basic morning routine, I brushed my hair so it no longer looked like a bird had made a nest in it overnight and it fell in its usual lifeless sheet down to my shoulders.

I got dressed in a simple long-sleeved white shirt, black zip-up hoodie, and the jeans that my mother had bought me for Christmas last year, claiming they hugged my curves. However, I was pretty sure they were nonexistent.

I was certain she only said it to try and make me feel better.

She got an A for effort though.

After slipping into my shoes, I did a once-over in the mirror to make sure I passed the acceptable-to-be-seen-by-society-today test, which really just consisted of me making sure I did not look like I had been living in a cave for the last three months before I went outside.

Satisfied with my look, I grabbed my backpack off the desk in the corner of my room and bounced down the stairs one at a time. I had tried the whole taking-two-steps-at-a-time thing once before, and let's just say my face had paid the price.

As soon as I reached the bottom step, the smell of bacon assaulted my nose, making my mouth water. Stepping into the kitchen, I saw my mom with her dark and slightly graying hair pulled into a messy bun still in her pajamas that was covered in bright yellow rubber ducks—a Christmas gift from yours truly—leaning over a frying pan full of bacon.

My dad, with his also graying black hair, was sitting on a chair at the kitchen table with a newspaper in one hand and a white "World's #1 Dad" mug—one of the many I had gotten him for three Christmases in a row—filled with coffee in the other. He looked like a dad straight out of a TV series.

Who even still reads newspapers these days?

He was dressed in a white button-up shirt and a black tie with purple polka dots—another Christmas gift from me—black slacks, and a pair of glasses were sitting on the bridge of his nose.

Walking over, I plucked two pieces of bacon off his plate and smiled sweetly at him as he looked up from his newspaper with his eyebrows raised.

"At your age, you shouldn't be eating this anyway," I said in response to his look as I shoved a piece into my mouth.

I walked over to my younger brother, Aiden, who was sitting on his highchair with a bowl full of—I eyed it skeptically—slop. It was definitely slop. I hoped he hadn't been eating that.

I ruffled his head full of fluffy brown hair before I leaned down and whispered in his ear, making sure I was still loud enough so that my parents could hear me clearly. "If you want to live to see three, you shouldn't eat that," I said, gesturing to the unidentifiable contents that I was pretty sure had just moved in his bowl.

In response to my whispered warning, Aiden smiled up at me like he knew exactly what I was talking about. My dad chuckled and my mom turned around to glare at me.

I shrugged and kissed her on the cheek before heading toward the front door. Before I opened it, I yelled over my shoulder, unable to stop myself. "Only eat the bacon! Anything else and you have two options: hospital or the grave!"

I quickly ran out the door before my mom could throw something at the back of my head, like the frying pan. I could hear my dad's laughter echoing outside before I quickly shut the door.

My mom would swear up and down that she was a good cook, but after last Thanksgiving, I begged to differ. That year, we had pizza for Thanksgiving after letting her try to cook. I thought that pretty much explained itself.

I couldn't help but laugh thinking about it. I then instantly checked my surroundings to make sure none of my neighbors were out and saw me laughing out here by myself. I continued munching on my last piece of bacon before I made my way down the sidewalk, the chilly air stinging my cheeks, and toward the subway, not knowing what exactly would be in store for me when I got there.

If you enjoyed this sample, look for
The Subway
on Amazon.

HER FINAL SORROW

FLORA McCONNELL

PROLOGUE

She runs towards me, fear in her eyes. I know what I need
to do.

I do what I should have done all along.
I lift my gun and I pull the trigger.
Death is a small price to pay for happiness.
And now, I finally am free.

ONE

Ava Milberry did not like to consider herself a divorcee. It was something that had never appealed to her, and as much as her seventeen-year-old self had believed in happily ever after, the divorce happened anyway. It wasn't as if it had come as a surprise to her, or that she had been cast aside by her husband after he had an affair with the young nanny. Her story wasn't dramatic, sad, or surprising. It was just a simple divorce. Mutual. Papers signed. House sold. *Simple.*

Ava certainly did not look back at her marriage with regret. How could she? Patrick brought her Mia, and she would never change that for the world. The one thing she did regret was selling her life away to her husband. Leaving her fun, single, university friends was a bad idea. Moving into Patrick's hometown was a bad idea. Becoming friends with Patrick's sister, Lily, was a bad idea. Selling her life to Patrick meant that now she no longer belonged to Patrick—that life was non-existent. They were Patrick's friends. It was Patrick's home. Lily was Patrick's sister, not Ava's best friend.

And so, she was lonely. Ava knew loneliness would be the first thing to creep in when the whole thing was said and done. Even when the marriage was on the rocks and she and Pat slept in different rooms, she was still married. She had someone to cook for. Someone to watch the evening news with. And now . . . she was divorced.

Being divorced put you in a whole new category of mothers. When Ava attended parent meetings, she would hear the question, "Will Mr. Milberry be joining us?"

She'd have to ruefully tell them that there was no Mr. Milberry. In fact, she was a single mother.

Despite that, Ava did not want to be married to Patrick anymore, she also did not want to be single. She couldn't remember what it was like to be single. Her last glimpse of being single was Freshers Week of university—where she managed to kiss a new boy every night. She doubted that single life in your late twenties was the same. A week into university and she met Pat. Her friends were envious; why wouldn't they be? She managed to tame Patrick Jules because he fell in love with her.

And now she was single. She often caught herself wishing she could go back in time and tell her twenty-year-old self to end the relationship while she still could. Immediately, she'd feel guilty because no Patrick meant no Mia.

And so, Patrick got to carry on living in Grennly with Ava's friends—ex-friends, it now seemed—who hadn't spoken to her since the divorce. She was now the ex-wife of the gorgeous and amazing Dr. Jules. Who would divorce such a man?

There wasn't anything wrong with Patrick. He was gorgeous, smart, funny, and an amazing father. But something had changed in him a year ago. It was as if he'd just fallen out of love with Ava, just like that.

Whilst Patrick's life had remained unchanged—apart from the fact the mothers from Grennly Park School for Infants would be fussing over the single, hot dad in town—Ava had to find a new town to settle into. There was no way Ava was going to stay in Grennly. She was going to find a new town and make new friends. She was going to start a new life.

It had been six months since the divorce was finalized. Six months since she left her life in Grennly. Six months living with her parents. And now there she was, sitting in her parents' sitting room, which smelled faintly of cigarettes even though her mother had sworn to give them up.

"There's no rush for you to move away, sweetie." Ava's mother, Carol, poked her head into the bathroom. Ava looked up from the bath where Mia squirmed about in the bubbles.

"Mia is turning five soon. Five means primary school," Ava told her mother bluntly. She had fond memories of her childhood home, but ever since returning, she could not wait to get her own life again. Having her parents around twenty-four-seven was far from ideal. Initially, it meant she had this newfound freedom. Now she felt constricted by their smothering and constant reminders that she *will* find another man.

"You could send her to school here. You've met some lovely women at the gym, haven't you? It isn't like you don't have friends here, sweetie," Carol insisted. Ava cast a bored look to her mother.

"Mum, I've found a house. Let me go live in it." Ava felt herself becoming irritated with her mother. She knew that she didn't visit her parents often when she was with Patrick, but things were different now.

"I'm just trying to help you, Ava." Carol's voice became sterner. Ava felt anger creeping up her spine. Her mother was acting as if she was a teenager again, telling her what to do. She seemed reluctant to accept that Ava had grown up and had a child—a child that needed a steady home.

"I know, Mum." She pushed the anger away. "But I don't want Mia to grow up in London. Plus, Tansbury is only an hour by train."

Tansbury was the town she had decided to reside in. It was a small town with one of the top primary schools in England. It was only short train ride to London. It sounded perfect.

Carol kneeled next to Ava and poured some shampoo into her hands. She gently applied it to Mia's wispy hair before speaking again, "Are you sure Tansbury is for you, Ava? It sounds remarkably similar to Grennly."

Ava knew this. She knew the sort of town she had landed herself into. Yummy mummies who were married to wealthy men, living in large houses that look like they should be in Beverly Hills. She loved her life in Grennly. She loved the people, the atmosphere, everything. So the fact that Tansbury was a clone of her ex-husband's town was some sort of victory.

"It's better for Mia that way," Ava said stubbornly before taking over Mia's bath time ritual. Carol looked slightly offended, because she knew this was the most she was ever going to be able to see her grandchild.

Carol didn't speak much more, and Ava was grateful. She was moving out to start her new life tomorrow. She had been given a clean slate and she sure as hell wasn't going to screw it up this time.

*　　*　　*

The next morning was how Ava expected it to be: stressful. She seemed to have had accumulated more clothes ever since staying with her parents. Mia wouldn't stop crying, Carol kept getting in the way, and Ava had to do all she could to not tell her to leave her alone. Her father, Oliver, was bumbling around with no direction, unsure of what to do with himself.

"Oliver, honey, have you put Mia's suitcase in the car?" Carol pestered her forgetful husband. Oliver looked blankly at his wife before shuffling to Mia's room to collect the fifth thing he had forgotten that morning.

"Mia, what's wrong?" Ava's daughter could not have picked a worse time to start crying.

"Mama, I want to see Daddy," she wept. Ava felt her stomach drop. The last time she had seen Patrick was a couple of weeks ago when he had dropped Mia off after their day at the zoo.

Patrick and Ava didn't speak much during the exchange, and she had felt as if she was involved in some sort of drug deal.

"Mama and Daddy are spending a little time apart. Okay, darling?" Ava used the same phrase she always used when Mia began to ask questions.

"I want to go home," Mia sobbed and Ava felt a pang of guilt. Why had she and Patrick not managed to sort out their differences? Why did they argue over everything?

"We're going to a new house, and you're having a Barbie room!" Ava tried to sound excited through her guilt. This idea seemed to perk Mia up, so much so that the crying stopped. This was a little victory for Ava, so she continued her packing of the car.

"Honey, are you sure about this?" Carol met her daughter at the car as she loaded the last suitcase into the boot. Ava inwardly rolled her eyes, but since she was leaving her mother for good, she decided not to treat her with tough love.

"I know this is hard for you, Mum. But I need to move on. I need a new life, okay? And I can't start one living under your roof." She placed her hand on Carol's arm. "You can come to visit whenever you want. I won't have my controlling husband there to stop you."

That comment made Carol laugh. She had never been particularly keen on her daughter's choice of husband, so when the divorce happened, she was secretly happy. She was not a fan of smug men, and Patrick was very smug indeed.

"I'm only a train ride away, sweetie. If you hate it—" she began, but Ava cut her off.

"I will be back in an instant. But Mum, I really think this is going to be good for me. I think I'm going to love it there." She pulled Carol into a hug and gave her a kiss on the cheek. Her father's goodbye was quiet and humble. She loved that about him; he knew what she wanted and always seemed to agree with her.

"Mia, let's get you strapped in." She placed her daughter in her booster seat and strapped her in. After double checking that she was safe, she bid her parents one last farewell before driving off to start her new life.

Ava was not used to driving in London; she and Patrick rarely visited since he was always busy in the hospital. She often wondered that if Patrick hadn't been a doctor, they might not have gotten divorced. But she cast away those thoughts because Patrick was a doctor and that wasn't going to change.

London was busy and the traffic made her grateful she wasn't staying with her mother any longer. This thought became especially prominent as she escaped the hustle and bustle of the city and entered the countryside.

"Where are we going, Mama?" Mia asked thoughtfully. Ava was relieved that her daughter had received her own personality traits rather than Patrick's. Patrick was charming, yes, but he was very arrogant. Her mother loved to point that feature out.

"To the Barbie house," Ava told her daughter happily. She *was* happy. She was going to live in a lovely white house in a lovely town with lovely people. She even allowed herself to think of the possibility of meeting someone new.

"Yay!" Mia had cheered up dramatically since their departure. She seemed to love being in the car, which Ava found very strange. Mia must have inherited that trait from her father.

As the miles on the road signs began to reduce, Ava felt herself becoming nervous to arrive in the new town. She began to worry about what the other mothers would think of her lifestyle. She wondered who, if any, the other single mothers would be. Would she be shunted to the side?

As the attempted to cast her negative thoughts aside, Ava nearly missed the turning. *Tansbury 2 miles.* Her heart leaped as the spun the steering wheel and turned onto the narrow road.

"We're nearly there, Mia!" Ava said, trying to push her anxiety away. Mia let out a little squeal excitedly. Within five minutes, the sat nav was telling Ava to turn into her new home. As they pulled onto the road, Ava spotted the house. She let out a little squeal herself. It was small, but perfect for the two of them.

"Here we are!" She pointed at the white house. Her daughter raised her sleepy eyes to the house, and they widened immediately.

"Barbie!" the little blonde girl yelped, and Ava let herself admire the house. For the first time in six months, she *let* herself be happy. The crushing pain from the divorce has lessened. No longer did she feel inadequate.

"Shall we go inside?"

*   *   *

Zoe: You there?
Louise: Yes.
Zoe: Do you think she did it?
Louise: Did who do it?
Zoe: You know who.
Louise: No, I don't. It must have been some sort of accident;
let's leave
it at that.
Zoe: That was not an accident, Lou.
Louise: Could have been. If it was her, she would be crazy.
I know
she's not crazy.

If you enjoyed this sample, look for
<u>**Her Final Sorrow**</u>
on Amazon.

THE

STRANGE

DISAPPEARANCE

OF

CALLA RIVERS

ANNE MARSHALL

Before

There was a chill in the night air as the leaves falling from the first changing trees of the season scattered along the sidewalk. They blew past house after house before settling in a pile against a thicket of bushes that the homeowner neglected. With the warmth of the clicking heater that needed tossing out years ago, the homeowner with the shaggy bushes sat among his deep thoughts with corn nuts scattered over his chest. Seemingly without a care in the world, he grunted and coughed up a few nuts before grabbing aimlessly for the remote stuck between him and the tattered leather armrest.

Flipping through the static-filled cable channels, the grimy homeowner breathed a deep sigh of relief. He didn't see any reporting on the abduction last night. His luck and attitude changed when the channels stopped on the twenty-four-hour news. He turned the volume up when he saw a familiar face plastered in the upper right corner that he wished he hadn't. Pausing and sitting forward, letting the nuts fall to the floor, he paid as much attention to the news as he could. Clicking the remote a few more times for the volume, he listened to what they had to say about the girl on his screen.

"Reports about a young coed that's been missing since last night have come in. Her parents called in a report that she ran away, but a witness might be able to shed some new light on the subject. More on the story at eleven. Until then, if you see a young woman, five feet eight, long brown hair, hazel eyes, and pale skin, please call your local police department. Her photo provided by her

parents is on the screen now. Any information is helpful. Now, onto the latest traffic report—"

He cut the TV off seconds after they changed the subject. He might not have been as careful as he thought. Cursing, he thought about the lies he would need to tell to get out of this situation. He couldn't run, not yet. He needed to bide his time until the coast was clear. This wasn't like the times before; they didn't have anyone looking for them. Why had he accepted this tempting offer? He knew it was too good to be true when he was given the information, but he took it anyway. One look at her and he fell harder than he ever fell before. He was promised that no one would be looking for her, that she was no one from a nothing family. The added information settled sourly in his stomach. He could hear the conversation with his supplier now. Pushing his fingers into his eyes until he saw only purple, he tried to think of something else.

No more than five minutes after the news report, a telltale sound came from the back bedroom. Clicking the TV back on, he turned the volume up until it drowned out the new noise. If his nosy neighbors reported him again, he would have to leave sooner, exposing himself and his project to the town—something he very much did not want to happen. The muffled sounds coming from the room started rising above the sound of the three stooges smacking each other on the television. Thinking on his feet, he decided to silence the noise the only way he knew how, without having to start the fun plans he had planned later.

Changing pace, he stood up from the ratty recliner and headed for the back room. Taking long strides down the short hall, the oily man threw the back bedroom door open and set his sights on the closet.

He stood at the front of the closet door while he listened to the pathetic moans and whimpers of the new project, the young lady that set his soul on fire when he looked into her begging eyes. He stood there for a moment and thought about that night. He thought of her pleading eyes, the ones swimming with wantoning need as her hands reached out for him, barely able to stand on her own feet without his help. The memory of her perfume engulfed him as it did that night. The scent of her sweat just under it—she had been dancing that night. He could even smell the vodka on her breath, remembering the drink he had spiced up for her at the club. It was only something to help her into his rough arms, nothing that would hurt her. He hated the idea of her being harmed in any way.

Breaking out of his memories when the sounds didn't stop, he banged on the door three times. When it finally died with a yelp, he turned to leave the room, but a sharp, piercing screech brought him to a full stop.

Turning back and making quick work of the small lock, he threw it on the bed behind him and slid the other locks out of place before pulling the door open.

Reaching for the lightbulb's string, he pulled on it until the yellow light was cast around the small room. Crouching down, he came face to face with his beloved new project.

"You're going to have to keep quiet. We wouldn't want to wake the neighbors, would we?" Lowering himself more, he reached out to touch the side of her face through the kennel bars, but she backed away as far as the metal cage would allow her to. He hummed to himself as he caught her hair between his rough fingers. His eyes lingered on the strands of deep brown hair as he curled them around his index finger. With the space of the walk-in closet, he had plenty of room to sit and stare at her all night, if he wanted. However, seeing the tears, dirt, and sweat on her face infuriated him. He wanted to clean her up and make her smile like he'd seen weeks ago when they first met. She didn't know him then, but when she smiled at him from across the room, he was consumed. It wasn't even just the tip about her existence from his buddy; she was truly a beauty, one that shouldn't be forgotten or wasted too quickly.

Tilting his head to the side, he opened the door to the kennel, just enough for him to reach in and hold her dirty face in his thick hand. Her eyes didn't meet his as they stayed stuck on the wall behind him. He shook her head until she squeaked and moved her eyes to look at his. "Good girl," he whispered as she flinched. He loved seeing the terror on her face. She was such a good actress, he believed. "Stay quiet and I'll give you a little treat." He twirled her hair again once his hand fell from her face.

"We're going to change a few things, dear. Don't worry, it won't hurt. I would never hurt you." With his unsettling grin, the fear that bloomed in her chest seeped into her soul. This wasn't a situation she was going to walk away from, that much she knew. Worse than that, she saw the empty void behind the man's eyes. Telling her every word that came out of his mouth would happen despite any effort she made to turn them into lies—to not believe in them. Hearing the news before told her everything she needed to know.

Breathing deeply, she closed her eyes as the kennel door closed and locked with a thick click. The last bit of hope that someone would come for her disappeared as she swallowed back the fear stuck in her throat. The light died around her as her mind searched for something to hold onto. With fuzzy thoughts, she reached for any sort of light still lingering inside her but found herself as dark as the closet. Her hope for survival was stuck in the room with her, hanging by a string of hope that frayed with every passing day.

If you enjoyed this sample, look for
The Strange Disappearance of Calla Rivers
on Amazon.

AUTHOR'S NOTE

Thank you so much for reading *A Deadly Trip*! I can't express how grateful I am for reading something that was once just a thought inside my head.

I'd love to hear your thoughts on the book. Please leave a review on Amazon because I just love reading your comments and getting to know you!

Can't wait to hear from you!

Jae Jae

ABOUT THE AUTHOR

Johnae' Jones (Jae Jae) is the author behind the first book in the short two book novel series "The Subway" which she started writing back during her Junior year in high school. Michigan born and raised, she now resides in Alabama where she attends school and devotes most of her time to writing and being a student.

Printed in Great Britain
by Amazon

45067576R00118